THE HAUNTING OF
LAMB HOUSE

THE HAUNTING OF LAMB HOUSE

Joan Aiken

St. Martin's Press
New York

Library of Congress Cataloging-in-Publication Data

Aiken, Joan
    The haunting of Lamb house / Joan Aiken.
        p.   cm.
    ISBN 0-312-09060-9
    1. Benson, Arthur Christopher, 1862-1925—Fiction.   2. James,
Henry, 1843-1916—Fiction.   3. Rye (England)—History—Fiction.
I. Title.
PR6051.I35H38   1993
823'.914—dc20   92-34392
                                                              CIP

First published in Great Britain by Jonathan Cape.

First U.S. Edition: January 1993
10 9 8 7 6 5 4 3 2 1

In memory of John Aiken
who lived in Rye and liked ghost stories

AUTHOR'S NOTE

All the characters and occurrences in these stories are entirely real (except, of course, for the ghosts and ghostly happenings, which are entirely invented, as is the whole of Toby Lamb's story).

Cognoscenti of Henry James and E.F. Benson will see that I have unabashedly made use of those writers' own words wherever possible. And I acknowledge a deep debt to the monumental biography of Henry James by Professor Leon Edel; to *Alice James: A Biography* by Jean Strouse; and to *E.F. Benson, As He Was* by Geoffrey Palmer and Noel Loyd; and to Mr and Mrs Martin for kindly allowing me to explore the attics and cellars and back regions of Lamb House.

The Stranger in the Garden

I · TOBY

MY SISTER ALICE left us when she was twelve, and was gone for eight years. As long as a lifetime, it seemed to me then, that absence of hers; and sadder events resulted from it than befall in many lifetimes. Yet it was agreed to, by my parents, for nothing but her good.

I can recall, as if it were yesterday, the moment when Alice came out to the little cobbled yard, her face all blubbered with tears, to tell me she must go. I (being but seven at that time and in poor health) was allotted such simple tasks as lay within my power. And on this chill, grey, wintry autumn afternoon, Grandmother Grebell had instructed me to turn the rushes that Gabriel the groom and my brother Robert had, several days before, brought in from the marsh, and to peel such of them as might be ready for it.

Rushlights are not so commonly used now, in these times of plenty, and you may see any artisan's home lit with wax candles; but my father, though a wealthy brewer and thirteen times Mayor of Rye, was always a frugal man. 'The marsh lies all about us,' I have heard him say, many a time, 'we are fools, and irreverent fools, if we do not make use of what God sends us.' And so the rushes that Robert and Gabriel fetched in had been set to soak in great tubs in the kitchen-yard, and it was my work to keep turning them, until they were softened, and then to strip off the peel from the stalks, leaving only one regular, narrow rib from top to bottom which would support the pith.—After which they must lie drying across racks of osier until they are ready to be dipped in scalding grease.

3

One pound of rushes thus prepared with six pounds of grease will give eight hundred hours' light, at a cost of less than three shillings.—So said my father, that careful man, and, as my hands worked at turning and stripping, my mind ran eagerly along its own track, reckoning that, if we had here ten pounds of rushes, that would allow us eight thousand hours of light ... how many days would that give, supposing we burned lights for five hours, evening and morning, in parlour, kitchen, and my father's office? Twenty pounds would give sixteen thousand hours ...

My thoughts at that time were greatly given to such games with figures and calculations. These cheered me through long and tedious tasks, peeling the rushes, scouring and oiling the harness of my father's mare and gig (for Gabriel the groom had plenty of other tasks, gardening, and my father's errands in the town). Perhaps, I thought, with longing and doubt, perhaps one day Father will send me to school.

'It is a pity not to have the boy taught, James,' I had heard Granny Grebell declare to him one day, in his counting-house. 'Toby has bright wits, and is willing.' (Although christened Thomas, I was always called Toby by my family.) 'He could be of value to you in the brewery, or here in the office.'

'Him? What use could he ever be?' My father sounded impatient and weary. 'A little sickly cripple? Now if only Robert—'

'Robert is a clod, and will never be more than a clod,' said my grandmother tartly; and then the door closed on their voices.

A rush snapped in my careless grip, and I flung it on to the growing pile of spoiled ones that would furnish kindling for the kitchen fire. Then I became aware of my sister Alice, running towards me across the cobbled court, her dark curls untidy, her face red and smeared with tears, her mouth open and sobbing.

'Oh, Toby! *Oh, Toby!*' She dropped down beside me, heedless of the wet rushes, or her linsey skirts, or the puddled water between the cobbles.

'*Alice?* What is it? Did you scald yourself? Did Robert hit you?'

Robert, not bad-tempered in general, could be passionate if crossed, only sorry when it was too late. 'Or did Father give you a scold?'

No rebuke would have come from our mother, I knew. She cared too little about her children to correct them, unless she found that somebody had disarranged her needlework. And Alice, good careful Alice, would never do that.

'N-no. Much, much worse! I am to go! I am to be sent away!'

'*Away?* From here? But where? But why?'

Here was my father's house in Rye. It was not conceivable to me that one might live anywhere else. And indeed I never have.

But Alice stumbled on with her tale, hicupping and sobbing.

'I am to go—to go to our cousin Honoria Wakehurst—at—at T-Tunbridge Wells. To live there.' From her voice it might as well have been Timbuktoo. And, so far as either of us knew, the two places might have been the same distance away. I gazed at Alice aghast, not yet believing or understanding what she said.

'But why? But I don't *want* you to go, Alice!'

Alice, from my earliest memories, had always been kind to me. Always, always. When I fell and hurt myself, when I was in disgrace, when I soiled my clothes, or spilled my food, or felt pain from my bad leg, Alice was always there, infallibly loving, infinitely comforting, gentle, patient.

'There, Toby, don't cry. Don't cry. Alice is here. Alice will make it better.'

She had been far more of a mother to me than our own mother ever was or would be. Now that I am old myself—I write this record more than sixty years after the events reported—now, I can understand that our mother was never in good health, often in much pain. She died of her complaint the year that Alice came home, when her last-born, our younger brother George, was only nine; and she must have been failing for years before that. During her lifetime we had learned to accept the fact that she spent her days on the sofa, doing her needle-work, and that all problems must be taken to Grandma Grebell, who, living just around the corner in Vicarage Lane, was in and out of Lamb House a hundred times a day.

I clung to Alice, repeating, 'I don't want you to go! I shan't *let* you go!'

'Little fool!' Stout eight-year-old Robert passed with a friend from the Grammar School and looked down at me scoffingly. 'Your face is all dirty,' he sneered at Alice, and, to me, 'How can *you* stop her going, crybaby? She is to go to Cousin Honoria and learn to be a grand lady. You'll never see her again. She will marry some rich merchant in Tunbridge Wells.'

And he went on his way whistling to ask Agnys the cook for a piece of bacon pudding, which she would undoubtedly give him.

'But why does Cousin Honoria Wakehurst want you, Alice? *This* is your home. I don't understand.'

'It is because she has no children of her own. And she is over thirty now, and probably can't have any. And she and Captain Wakehurst are rich. Father says it will be a fine thing for me.'

'But why would they want a girl?'

Even I, at seven, knew that girls had small value beside boys.

Alice gave a great sniff, gulped, and said, 'Oh, of course they would rather have had a boy. But Father would never part with Robert. And Moses is too small, only two. And—'

She stopped. But I knew what she meant. Nobody in their senses would wish to adopt *me*, crippled, undersized, and with my other misfortune. That none of it was my own fault, I understood, but such understanding made it no easier to bear.

Grandmother Grebell came into the yard. Her sharp wrinkled face, grown even sharper since she lost her teeth, pointed down at us like that of an old hound.

'Toby, you have done your task very ill! What a deal of rushes you have spoiled and broken! But now it is time for you to come indoors. And you too, Alice. We must look through all your clothes to see what will be fit to take away with you. Child! Don't begin shedding tears again, over what can't be mended. Put a brave face on it.'

'But I am *not* brave,' said Alice simply.

She was not, I knew. Many things terrified her—snarling dogs, thunder, loud noises, angry voices, the sight of blood; I did not see how she would ever manage, away from our familiar, safe life at Lamb House.

Grandma Grebell frowned at me over Alice's heaving shoulders.

'Toby: go quickly to the herb garden—' (she did not say *run*, for I could not)—'and fetch a bundle of mint. It is withered, but still has some fragrance, better than what is dried. I shall make you a tisane, miss,' she said, fixing Alice with a gimlet eye, 'and you will go to bed, and in the morning you will accept your future with a good grace, as befits your grandfather's grandchild.' (Grandfather Grebell had fought bravely at the Battle

7

of Blenheim, and become Mayor of Rye the following year.)

'Yes, grandmother,' said Alice, sobbing, and followed the old lady into the kitchen.

I limped my way across the cobbled yard, along the narrow lane, past the brewery wall, and into the little enclosed garden-space, where there were a few ancient apple trees, and a mulberry that my father had planted, and Gabriel, as well, cultivated parsley, onions, and pot-herbs. With a heavy heart I peered about in the early dusk and picked a few handfuls of mint, withered now, but still sweet-smelling. Then I turned to make my way back to the house.

Surprised, I observed a stranger by the gateway—a tall person, all in black like a priest, black stockings and shoes, a square boxlike black cap, and a big caped cloak thrown like a wing over his right shoulder.

'S-Sir?' I stuttered, taken quite aback. 'Do you seek my f-father? Mr James Lamb?'

But, even more puzzling, the strange gentleman neither answered nor looked at me, only passed silently and rapidly out of the little garden. Furthermore, when I reached the doorway in the wall, and looked either way for him, he was not to be seen, though I did not understand how he could have got away so swiftly. Still, he was gone, and I soon forgot him, overwhelmed by this woe of parting from Alice. How could I bear it if she went away? Alice was more than half my world. Robert never paid any heed to me, nor did my father, except to look at me sometimes as if he was sorry I had ever been born. The younger ones, Sophy and Moses, were too small to be company, and George, the littlest of all, was only a few months old. George had been born last winter, and great commotion attended his birth, for that night, in a wild raging storm, the King himself, returning from Hanover, had his ship

blown ashore in Rye Bay, and was obliged to walk from Jury's Gap and take shelter in the town. My father, as Mayor, must invite His Majesty to stay with us, and turn out of his own bedroom; very inconvenient this invasion was, for the King spoke only German, and so did most of his servants. My father, not having any German, was forced to send round the corner for Dr Wright, who had studied medicine in the Low Countries, to interpret for the royal party. (And there was little love lost between Father and Dr Wright over the affair, six years earlier, of my own misfortune.)—Added to that, during the night, our mother, disturbed by all the excitement, had given birth, prematurely, to my brother George. (So he was christened, though we all called him Jem.) He himself had done best out of the episode for the King, obliged to remain in the town for three days until the storm abated, had stood godfather, and later a handsome silver bowl came down from London, inscribed 'King George to his godson George Lamb.' I used to gaze at the bowl wistfully, sometimes, where it stood in the parlour, and wonder why some were born to be lucky and others, i seemed, to unremitting misfortune.—Of course, during th royal visit, *I* was obliged to keep in the kitchen well out sight . . .

'*Toby!*' called my grandmother in exasperation. 'H will you, boy, with that mint!'

'Here it is, ma'am—'

Grandma, with a jug of boiling water at han endeavouring to cheer my sister by recalling a Tunbridge Wells that she had taken with o grandmother, years ago.

'In those days, my dear, it was but a litt place, for Lord North had not long previously the healing spring. There was a shabby inn, a hill, and that was all; but now 'tis a fine th

there will be shops, and Assembly Rooms, libraries, bands playing and regiments quartered; in a year or so I daresay Cousin Honoria will begin taking you to balls; why, you are the luckiest girl in Rye! Now, don't show me that sulky face, or they will be sorry they didn't pick Sophy, though she is only four—'

'I wish they had!'

'Drink your drink, miss, and go to bed,' snapped grandmother, suddenly at the end of her patience. 'You look like a gaby! A great girl of your age to let her face get swelled up with weeping in such a foolish manner! What will Captain Wakehurst think when he comes tomorrow? Run along with you, now.'

Alice, indeed, as (having swallowed the potion) she crept away, looked more dead than alive. Her normally smooth brown-and-pink complexion was blotched with red, her face, never pretty but at all times sweet and friendly, was completely swollen out of shape, and the beautiful dark-brown eyes half hidden under inflamed shiny lids; her soft dark hair was dank and draggled, all out of curl. Alice was at that time chubby, not tall; she would never win acclaim for her swanlike shape or elegance of deportment; but there was something very taking to the eye and comfortable about the way in which her plump arms and legs tapered to small neat hands and feet; her hands, indeed, were so tiny and tender-looking that any stranger might wonder at their capacity for hard work. Already at twelve she was a notable housewife and manager, undertaking many of the duties that my mother found herself unable to perform.

'We shall miss her sadly, I don't deny,' sighed my grandmother, as Alice went hiccuping away up the back stairs. 'Who is to make the butter now I'm sure I can't imagine; Agnys will never have time, and Polly is too needless—'

I was concerned with something Grandmother had said earlier.

'Cousin Honoria Wakehurst is coming here *tomorrow*? So soon as that?'

'Aye, child, before winter sets in and the roads grow too bad. And, as matters are, it's as well; the girl will only cry herself sick from now until she goes, so Dr Betimes will make the best physician. Once she is with them, she will become accustomed to their ways; the town will have distractions to take her mind away from memories of home . . . Don't look at me with those great eyes, child—!'

I said, slowly, hardly believing it, 'So, by tomorrow this time, Alice will be gone . . .'

Tears were not my habit. Perhaps because, from infancy, I had the pain of my lame leg, and other troubles beside, to contend with; I had become used to bear my afflictions as best I could on my own.

My grandmother knew this and laid a hand gently (for her) on my head.

'Toby, try not to grieve. I know Alice has been the sun and the moon for you, but sooner or later you would have had to learn to live without her. In four or five years she would have married, in any case—such a famous little housewife as she is—then she would be gone from you—'

'She said she would have me to live with her! In Look-Out Cottage! She said so, often.'

'Then she made a very rash, foolish promise. Suppose her husband would not agree?'

'Then she would not have married him.'

'Girls have little choice in these matters!' snapped Granny Grebell, who had gone back to her constant occupation of spinning, and was punching the treadle of the spinning-wheel with her foot, and furiously twisting the bank of raw wool with her fingers, as if by doing so she could flatten and demolish all contrary argument.

'By moving to Tunbridge Wells, she may do better for herself. She will have more choice, she will live like a lady, for the Wakehursts have many friends, and are wealthy—'

'So is my father.'

'Yes; but here, Alice had all the brood of you younger ones to care for. With them, she will be the only young one, indulged and pampered—'

Did my grandmother say these things in order to reassure herself? We knew little about these Wakehursts, who had been abroad with the Captain's regiment until lately.

Granny went on, 'You should be glad, for Alice's sake, and not find fault with her chance to better herself. And for you, too, it may be a lucky turn. You have lived always in her shadow; now you will be obliged to fend for yourself.'

That sounded like a wretched prospect to me. Without Alice, how should I survive? Robert was rough and indifferent; he and I never had any liking for each other, our habits were too dissimilar. The younger ones, Sophy and Moses, despised me, because I could not play their scampering games; also I made them nervous; my disability depressed them, they were never easy in my company; and Jem was only a baby.

'If my father would only send me to school,' I muttered.

'I fear he will never do that.' Granny did not descant on what I was perfectly aware of: my father, who had a very cheese-paring streak (as, I daresay, all rich men do) did not expect that I would live to maturity, consequently he refused to spend a penny on my education. In extenuation he said that, lame and crippled as I was, I would never be able to fend for myself at the Grammar School, which may have been true. From various muttered remarks that Grandmother Grebell had let fall, at various times, I knew that it was my father's thriftiness I had to thank for my lame and deformed condition. If he had ensured that a proper practitioner, or even apothecary, had been in attendance, instead of a drunken midwife, at the hour of my birth; if he had hired that same Dr Wright (with whom he was on such poor terms because of what he considered the doctor's extortionate bills) instead of old Mrs Tubsey who, after numerous potations of gin, had accidentally set fire to my cradle-clothes—

'Your father is a hard man to manage, child. But managed he must be; only it has to be done advisedly, with cunning and forethought.'

That (for some reason) reminded me of the man I had seen while picking mint.

'Grandmother, I forgot to say, there was a person in the garden; I suppose, seeking my father. I asked him, but he made no answer to me.'

'A person, child? What kind of a person?'

I tried to remember. Already the details were fading in my mind.

'Well, he wore a black cloak. A long one, somehow tossed up on his shoulder. And, I think, a square hat, very odd in shape. I never saw his face. And he made no answer when I called to him—'

The spinning-wheel had creaked to a halt. Granny Grebell stared at me in silence. Her face had blanched whiter than the frilled cap she wore.

After a moment's pause she said, first working her jaw as if to swallow,

'Where did you see this—person?'

'In the little garden. But then he walked out through the door, and he was gone when I followed into the lane—though I went as fast as I could—'

'I am sure you did, child,' she said absently. 'But he would always be gone—'

13

'Grandmother, *who was it?*'

But she suddenly grew angry, refusing to answer questions, exclaiming that it was late, disgracefully late, I should have been in my bed an hour since, for there would be much to do in the morning, the Wakehursts were expected for breakfast, they would want more than bread-and-cheese and beer, and Alice must be prepared and ready to leave directly after.

Utterly quenched by this prospect I crept up the narrow back stairs to my cot in the attic bedroom I shared with Moses and Robert. Our sisters had the next attic; the other two were occupied by menservants and maidservants respectively; Jem the baby still slept on the floor below with our mother.

Sophy, who should have been long asleep, came pattering in, to announce, 'Alice wants you, Toby!'

I went into the girls' room, the skylight of which faced eastwards up Vicarage Lane, past the solemn stare of the church, and over the red, jumbled roofs of the town towards Playden village.

Alice was huddled miserably on her bed, surrounded by a tangle of her possessions: mittens, cotton stockings, a straw hat, calico patches, a pair of garden clogs. The rush portmanteau in which these things would travel stood nearby on the floor.

'Toby,' she said, in a voice faint and worn from weeping, 'you may have my window-eye. It would be childish to take such toys where I am going.'

She gazed at me in a kind of prophetic fear. Many times, since, I have remembered that look on her poor swollen face.

I protested: 'But, Alice, you will want your nice things to remind you of home. And the eye is so beautiful!'

'No, brother Toby!' squeaked Sophy, who was dancing about, clasping, I now observed, Alice's treasured wooden doll, Lucy, given her on her fourth birthday by our Uncle Allen. Hitherto Sophy had never been allowed to touch this doll. 'See, she has given me Lucy! Because, where she is going, you may be sure, she will have all manner of fine things.'

'Take the eye, Toby,' Alice said tiredly. 'And may it bring you luck. It has brought me none.'

She handed me the eye, which was in reality the central whorl from a broken glass window-pane. Our uncle Jonas Didsbury, a builder and glazier by trade, gave it to Alice long ago, and for years it had been one of her greatest treasures.

I took the green, shining thing and looked into its curving depths.

'I will keep it safe for you, anyway, Alice, till you come back.'

'I shall never come back,' she said.

And there, I do believe, she spoke the truth.

'Oh, Alice, dear, *dear* Alice!' I cried out in a lamenting tone. 'I will quickly learn to write, and then I shall be able to write and tell you what is happening at home. I almost know the letters already, from Robert's bricks. I *will* write you, I promise!'

'What is the use of that?' replied her weary voice, 'when I shall not be able to read what you write?'

Alice had never shown much aptitude for learning to read or write. And, latterly, she had been too much occupied with household tasks to have time to spare for any schooling.

'Cousin Honoria is sure to have you taught,' I told her hopefully. 'You will soon be a learned lady and will read Latin and Greek.'

'Are you mad? More likely I shall be making jellies in the still-room.'

Polly the maid blew in like a whirlwind.

'All you young ones will get a strapping if you are not in your beds directly. Yes! Even you, miss!' she said to Alice, who lay down among her belongings with an indifferent shrug, as if she did not care what happened.

I said, 'Goodnight, Alice. I will take great care of your eye,' and went back to my own room which looked over the dark marsh to the faint lights of Winchelsea, and where Robert and Moses were already asleep.

Next morning the Wakehursts arrived before breakfast was ready (my grandmother had been in the house since five o'clock harrying the maids to prepare a meal of so many dishes that it more resembled dinner than breakfast) so Robert and I were instructed by my father to escort Captain Wakehurst to see the sights of the town. He had not visited Rye before, he told us, since his regiment had been, until recently, on garrison duty in Gibraltar. He thought Rye a handsome town—as indeed it is. I love it to this day, so warm and welcoming as it always appears, with its fine redbrick houses snuggled together on the hill.

Robert was always running ahead, leaping over mounting-blocks, climbing steps on to lookout walls, disappearing down narrow alleyways, or springing up gangplanks to talk to his cronies; so it fell to me to tell our guest about the market place, the town well, the harbour-side, with a French ship unloading, and the walls, with the entry where the Postern gate had lately been removed, now there was no longer any fear of a French invasion.

Captain Wakehurst seemed only moderately interested in the things I had to tell him.

Wine was unloading from the French ship, and he remarked, 'I daresay there's many a cask comes in here that never pays duty, hey?'

'As to that I could not say, sir,' I replied.

On our return up steep Mermaid Street, my lame leg dragging, despite all my efforts, he said in a sneering voice,

'I am happy to apprehend that your sister Alice has two good legs, not a leg and a twig, like you. Tell me about her. Is she a succulent little duckling, like the rest of the Rye girls?'

I had observed how he cast a number of glances at the young girls that we passed, and favoured many of them with smiles and winks.

'I cannot say, sir. I suppose she is well enough,' I told him doubtfully.

'*Well enough!* Does she have a whole troop of suitors, lads of the town who are mad after her and sigh under her window of an evening?'

'Indeed she does not!' I answered rather indignantly. 'Firstly my father would not allow it. And secondly, Alice is much too busy in the house to be caring a farthing for such foolery—'

'Ay, ay,' he returned with some complacence. 'I understand that she is a notable little housewife.'

'—And thirdly,' I added with triumph, 'no one could sing under her casement, for she sleeps with Sophy in the attic, and it has only a skylight.'

At that Captain Wakehurst burst into a great shout of laughter and told me that I was a bright young shaver, brighter than my looks gave me credit for. He then rammed a hand into his tight breeches pocket and found a sixpence, which he bestowed on me, saying that he knew my father was a sad old miser who probably never allowed me a bent penny to spend on myself.

Although this was partly true, I did not care for Captain Wakehurst, and was reluctant to take his money. But he pressed it into my hand and then, Robert belatedly catching up with us, red-faced and short of breath, said to me, laughing, 'It shall be a secret between us, eh? And we'll not tell your brother—' giving Robert a mocking glance. Which greatly provoked Robert, who stared at the two of us in dismay, wondering what he had missed.

—I have not described Captain Wakehurst. He was a tall, plump man, very fashionably dressed, with a somewhat sallow face, black sharp eyes, and bushy black brows which seemed ill-suited to the wig he wore. He laughed often, displaying large white teeth. He appeared younger than my cousin Honoria, whom I did not remember (though she said we had met when I was younger) and treated her with very little respect. She was talking with my parents in the parlour when we returned, and gave me a sad puzzled glance, which troubled me, until I came to realise that was the only look her face ever wore. She was a haggard-looking lady, but rigged out very fine, her wide skirts covered with a frilled and pleated overdress, her hair piled high and ornamented with velvet fruits. Our mother looked a plain dowd beside her, and I fell into a worry lest Alice should seem too poor and humble when she appeared; but when she did come slowly in with her gaze fixed on the floor, I saw that Granny Grebell had made over an old blue chintz gown of my mother's for her, and Polly had curled her hair in ringlets, with gauze ribands and a little lace cap. So that although Alice crept in very shyly, and never spoke, except to make her greeting, she did not look as I had feared she might, and I saw both Cousin Honoria and Captain Wakehurst give her several approving glances, especially the latter.

'And so this is to be our little new daughter,' observed Cousin Honoria in her high, fatigued voice, and then resumed talking to my mother about the extortionate cost of hair powder and the impossibility of finding tolerable servants in Tunbridge Wells. 'So different from Gibraltar!'

My father, I thought, seemed impatient. He was dressed fine enough, for the occasion, in the grey cloth jacket and waistcoat that he kept for his mayoral ceremonies; his stockings and cravat were of the whitest and he had on his silver-buckled shoes. But he looked as if he wished the occasion were well over.

Breakfast was speedily eaten, for the journey home would take them three hours or more, and the Wakehursts wished to leave without delay. I could eat nothing and nor, I saw, could Alice.

Our cousins' coach waited at the bottom of the hill, since Captain Wakehurst said he would not walk his horses over those cobbles for all the tobacco in Virginia. So the whole family went down to the bottom of the street in a straggling group, and I kept close beside Alice. What could we say? There was nothing to be said. I could not tell her, 'You will soon be home again', for she would not. Nor was I able to say, 'I shall come and visit you', for I had no power to do so. I tucked the sixpence Captain Wakehurst had given me into the little silken purse that hung on her wrist. 'Here is sixpence, *dear* Alice; you may find that you need to buy something—' but she never even asked how I had come by it, though it was the first sixpence I had in my life.

Captain Wakehurst lifted her into the coach, laughing, and declaring that she weighed no more than a Yarmouth herring. 'We shall soon fatten her up!' he told my father, who was looking at his watch as if he could not wait to get back to the brewery and his normal day's work. Our mother, who had played little part in the proceedings, took one of her dizzy spells and had to be helped back up the hill by my uncle Allen Grebell who happened to come past just at that moment. (I noticed the Wakehursts give him somewhat scornful glances.) My Uncle Allen was never a man to trouble about his appearance overmuch: his chocolate-coloured suit looked rusty, his wig was unpowdered, his shirt-neck and the knees of his breeches were loose, his black worsted stockings wrinkled, and his shoes unpolished. He carried a book and read in it as he walked. Yet he was alert enough in assisting my mother, when he saw her need.

'Goodbye, goodbye!' shouted the little ones, Sophy and Moses, jumping up and down waving their kerchiefs. Alice in the coach was hardly visible, just a pale portion of her face at the window.

'I won't *want* Alice to go!' wept Sophy suddenly, beginning to realise her loss, but by then the whip had cracked and the horses had broken into a trot.

I walked back up the hill beside my father, holding the hands of the little ones, feeling my heart as heavy and cold as the round flint cobbles under my feet.

The day, which had begun badly, continued worse. A fine, sleety rain set in, thickening to a downpour, and the wind rose to gale force, hustling and muttering in the chimneys, roaring and rocking over the roofs of the town. Our house (which my father had built only five years earlier, on the site of a much older one) seemed marvellously snug and secure with its thick panelled walls and well-made sash windows. But I thought of those poor travellers battling their way through the storm; where would they be by now? Somewhere in the forested Weald; perhaps, I hoped, the gale did not blow so hard there, amongst the trees; gentle timid Alice, like my mother, hated wind and stormy weather, the howl of the blast made her flinch and cry out. How would she be faring now, with those two strangers, in the carriage, so far away from all she knew? It seemed wrong, selfish almost, to be taking advantage of the warmth and comfort here in our house, and I would have shifted further from the fire, but I was holding wool for Granny Grebell as she wound it, and so could not move.

'Where do you think they may be by now, ma'am?'

'Oh . . . Lamberhurst, perhaps, if their horses go stead-ily; but your Uncle Allen did not think much of Captain Wakehurst's eye for horseflesh: flashy but not good goers, your Uncle Allen said.' A dry sniff. '*His* eye roves else-where, plainly.'

'What do you mean, Grandma?'

'Never mind what I mean, boy; there! Now fetch me the other hank from the window-seat. Lord save us! What's that?'

A frightful cry had come from upstairs, from my mother's chamber, where she had retired towards dusk, complaining of pains in her legs and head. As these troub-led her frequently and were nothing out of the common, no one had paid her any heed. But now she was calling out like a possessed creature: 'Come, oh please come! Come *quickly*! Bring a light, bring lights!'

Polly and Agnys were there almost at once, Grand-mother close behind them, panting up the stairs, and I as soon after her as I could manage it.

'What is it, ma'am?'

'What ails you, daughter?'

'Mother, what's the matter?'

The maids had rushlights with them; Polly threw a bit of wood on the fire, causing it to blaze up.

My mother was leaning up against her pillows, a cloud of hair escaping from under her cap, her eyes mere black pools of shadow in the uncertain light.

'Oh, I had such a terrible dream. I shall never dare to go to sleep again—never!'

She stared wildly round the room, which was known to us as the 'King's Room', for that was where King George had slept on the snowy night when my brother was born. It, like my sisters' attic above, faced eastwards up Vicarage Lane, and as we clustered round my mother's bedside, the church clock boomed out the hour of nine.

21

'But what was the dream about, ma'am? Tell us—then you'll feel better,' counselled Agnys the cook, a fat, kindly woman with a hare-lip who had been with the family since I was born.

'Oh I could never do that—it was by far too horrible,' said my poor mother with another shudder.

I heard the front door slam below. My father had been over at the brewery, checking around his mash tubs to see they were all at the right temperature, as he did always at this hour.

'Hallo—Agnys—Polly—where is everybody?' I heard him call, and then, hearing our voices I suppose and seeing lights, he came upstairs.

'What's amiss?' he called.

Grandmother went out to talk to him in the hall and I heard her say something about the doctor.

'Fiddlestick!' said my father. 'A dram of brandy is all she needs. Polly! Fetch your mistress a dram directly—' and he came into the bedroom, scattering us, giving me a look of sharp displeasure. 'Toby—what are you doing here in your mother's chamber? Be off—go and find yourself some useful occupation.'

'I was helping Grandmother wind wool, sir, until—'

'Oh, very well, very well,' he said impatiently. 'Where is Robert?'

'Round at the house of Tom Swayne, sir, in Mermaid Street.'

At this a cloud of vexation crossed my father's brow, but he only repeated, 'Well, be off,' and I was glad enough to escape. I went shivering down to the kitchen where a hearty fire burned and Agnys, likewise sent downstairs by my father, was talking in a low tone to the menservants Gabriel and Dickie. I could hear snatches of the conversation, and make out that it related to dreams and omens—'A great white dog running across the marsh—' 'owlets hooting in

Dead Man's Lane—' 'saw it in the grave-yard, plain as I see you—' then, becoming aware of my presence, they fell silent, and Agnys remarked kindly, 'You look pale and grievous, Master Toby, and you never touched your dinner, that I saw. Would you like a piece of cake, now, or a sup of gruel?'

'No, thank you, Agnys.' Then I asked, 'Do you think my cousins with Alice will have got to Tunbridge Wells by now?'

'Lord bless you, yes, long ago, child! Why, your sister Alice will be sleeping snug as a dormouse, this very minute, under silk sheets and velvet covers.'

Slightly cheered, not by the statement itself, which for some reason I found hard to believe, but by the kindly spirit that prompted it, I was emboldened to ask about another matter which had been puzzling me, under my grief.

'Agnys, who *was* the stranger in the garden yesterday? Grandmother Grebell never did tell me.'

And of course I would never have dared ask my father.

'Stranger in the garden, child? What stranger?'

They all exchanged looks. Both men were staring at me now, as well as Agnys.

'The strange man I saw last night in the black hat. In the garden. Did he come to see my father?'

'Saints preserve us!' whispered Agnys. 'The boy's seen the Frenchman!'

She made the sign of the cross, and so did Gabriel.

'Frenchman? What Frenchman?'

The name stirred some dimly-apprehended memory in me. I had heard it before, but always in low tones, whispered, not meant for my ears.

I noticed Polly exchange some signal with the two men. Gabriel said, 'Well: since the boy's *seen* it, after all—'

'I know, but master forbids us to be talking of such

23

things with the children—he'd be in a rare taking—'

I cried out in sudden enlightenment, 'Do you mean it was a *ghost*?'

My father was strongly opposed to all kind of talk about superstitions and spectres; he said, truly enough I daresay, that servants and vulgar persons exaggerated such stories and made much of them, to frighten themselves, and because they had idle minds and little else to think about. It was not, I was sure, that he himself entirely disbelieved such tales, rather that he did not think them proper matter for servants' gossip.

Now, out came the story of the Frenchman, in its various versions.

'It was over a hundred year ago, maybe two,' said Agnys. 'When a great number of French would be coming to Rye from the port of Dieppe to escape from the Papists who persecuted them. Frenchmen of the Reformed Religion, that is. Many were weavers or spinners, or connected with the wool trade, that was why they came to Rye.'

'And there was one called Andrew Morel,' put in Gabriel.

'Francis, *I* heard it,' corrected Dickie.

'What matter the name, Francis or Andrew?' said Agnys crossly. 'He was a weaver, very skilled, and he found lodging with a cloth-merchant, Thomas Harrold, in Watchbell Lane. Thomas had a sister, Margrat, who lived with him and kept house, and she was a weaver too; the Frenchman got friendly with her, and taught her many new patterns, and at first her brother was pleased that it should be so. But then, and it's not to be wondered at, the young couple, seeing each other every day, working so close together, became fond; and the Frenchman asked Thomas for Margrat's hand in marriage. That made Thomas angry, for his sister was useful to him, he did not wish to lose her, especially, he said, to a beggarly Frenchman with no home or country of his own. So he forbade the match, and turned Morel out of doors.'

'And what happened then?'

'The young couple went on meeting in secret. There used to be orchards, at the back of Watchbell Lane, where your pa's brewery now stands—that's where they met.'

'And?'

'Thomas learned that they still met, and was even angrier. He had information conveyed to the magistrates that Morel was really a secret agent of the French government.'

'A spy!'

'There was war with France at that time,' Agnys explained, and we all nodded. There usually was war with France, and Rye had been sacked and burned by the French at least twice.

'Orders were laid to arrest Morel. But somebody warned him in time. And he would have escaped and gone over to the Low Countries—for there were many more ships leaving Rye Harbour in those days—but the girl, Margrat, sent him word that she must see him one more time. Maybe she wanted to give him a keepsake.'

'And?'

'They did meet the one more time, but that was their undoing, for Morel was taken, and tried (some said that her brother had forced her to arrange the meeting) and he was hanged as a spy.'

'Drawn and quartered too, it's said,' remarked Dickie with relish.

'Was he really a spy?'

'Who can say? It's over, long long ago.'

'What happened to Margrat?'

'She died of grief—' Polly was beginning, 'or made away with herself, some say she swallowed a powder of ground-up glass—'

Gabriel struck in. 'Nay, that's not it. She had a child—or was to have one; and her brother had her walled up, child and all; folk could hear the ghost of the child crying for twenty year after, I've heard tell, till Vicar came with candle and censor and blessed the spot—'

'Hold your hush, Gabriel Roben!' broke in Agnys, giving him a furious, quelling look. 'If master were to hear you—! Besides, that's not the true story! That's the story of the monk and the young lady—'

They would have started arguing about it, but just then my brother Robert came sneaking in by the back entry, from which the alley led on to Mermaid Street. His clothes were soaked through, his hair hung down in points, he was draggled with mud, and it was plain that he had *not* been virtuously reading Latin with his friend Tom Swayne, but out doing something disreputable in the streets. Unfortunately for him, at this moment my father appeared to say that, because of my mother's continuing distress, my grandmother would be passing the night with us, and Polly must make him up a bed in a guest chamber. His full wrath fell upon Robert, but he spared a part of it to order me off to bed.

That night I hardly slept. I could well understand what my poor mother meant when she said, 'I shall never dare to go to sleep again!' Every time I drifted into slumber, I was assailed by such terrible dreams that I shot upright in bed, trembling like a leaf, pushing the dark away with my hands. It was no comfort to hear the church clock telling its steady march through the hours of dark. There were too many of them. The night seemed to go on for ever.

Sometimes I thought I could hear Margrat's baby crying inside the wall. Sometimes the voice was that of my sister Alice, caught up in a web of dire, unthinkable pain and fear. Sometimes it was my mother, calling out in terror, 'There is a stone in place of my heart. Here! You

can feel it! He has taken out my heart and left a stone in
its place.'

Once I really did hear my mother cry out, 'Alice!
Alice!' and I pattered barefoot down the stairs in terror,
but found my grandmother, formidable in her nightcap
with a lighted candle at the bedside, who told me to
make haste back to my own room. So back I went, to
lie awake, wondering. Was my mother really so attached
to Alice? Was Alice's loss such a grievous blow to her?
I had never seen signs of any great affection—but then,
who knew what my mother felt at any time? She was not
a gentle person, she had quarrelled bitterly with my Uncle
Allen's wife Catherine Hodges, and the two women had
not spoken for fifteen years, though living on opposite
sides of the street. At Aunt Catherine's death, a year
previously, Mother had said, 'Thank God for that. Now
he's free,' and then never alluded to my aunt again. What
she felt for Alice, who knew?

True it was, though, that from the day of Alice's going,
my mother's final decline set in, slow but steady; even if
few took note of it at the time.

Next morning I seized a moment when Agnys was
hanging out clothes on the line and I was chopping
kindling-wood to ask her,

'Was that really the end of the story, Agnys? About
the Frenchman and Margrat?'

'Bless you, yes, child—so far as I know. But it's all
different tales that people tell. Some say one thing and
some another.'

'Well then—why does the Frenchman come back?
Because he never saw his lover? To leave her a message? Or because she was going to give him a keepsake?'

'Maybe so,' said Agnys. 'In hopes of seeing her, one
last time, poor devil. Or some do say that "the man in

black" is really Margrat in boy's disguise, come to meet her sweetheart.'

'Oh, no.' I reconsidered the meeting in the little garden. 'No, I'm as certain as can be that it was a man.'

Agnys looked at me, I thought, queerly.

'Are you so? Well, there's one thing you can be sure of then, Master Toby.'

'What's that, Agnys?'

'The Frenchman left a curse when he died. Or'—Agnys revised her phrasing—'a kind of warning, some would say. "I die innocent," says he. "And I wish on any who come after me, any who see me walk the streets of this town, a long life—" '

'But that's not a curse,' I said. 'That seems a good wish, Agnys. Who'd mind that?'

'Wait, I haven't finished yet.' Agnys went on with some reluctance. ' "I die young," says Morel, "but there's worse fates than to die young. It's worse to die old, and never have done what you most wish. May any soul who meets me have a long life and a hollow one, empty for ever of his dearest hope. May he always seek and never never find," says Morel. And after that he died.'

Well, thought I, is that such a dire fate to lay on anybody? Who in this world really knows what he wants most of all? And who really receives it? What do I wish for, most in this world? I want my sister Alice back; and that happiness I know I shall not have. And what else do I want?

'What became of Thomas Harrold, Agnys?'

'He lived to be old and rich. Never married. Left no heir. So all his money went to the town treasury.'

'I wonder what *he* wanted most?'

'Come to me directly, Agnys, I want you to help me turn the mistress's mattress,' called my grandmother. 'And, Toby, child, I've a task for you; take this pair of your father's boots to the shoe-mender; and don't dawdle about it, but hurry back, for I wish you to polish all the lamps and their chimneys.'

My grandmother kept me busily occupied all that day; as soon as one piece of work was completed she found me another; I am sure she meant it kindly, so that I should not be given time to think and grieve too much; nonetheless I *did* think and *did* grieve; often, as I cleaned the dribbled wax off a pair of brass candlesticks, ready to be melted down and made into new candles; or scraped the moss from between the pebbles of the little kitchen-yard, or mended a basket with bits of osier, or turned the apples on the shelves of the shed and picked out any that had spots of decay (to be made into jelly; nothing in our house went to waste) the tears would, in spite of my best efforts, keep flooding into my eyes, and I must blink and swallow many times, to prevent myself from breaking down like a baby.

I thought of gentle Alice, shy and confused among wealthy strangers. My thoughts ran like wheels in a stony groove, and I could not stop them. Alice was, at all times, somewhat slow of speech; her thoughts did not readily assemble themselves into words; whereas I had seen that my cousin Honoria and her husband were quick-witted and quick-spoken worldly people who rattled out ideas and comments like hailstones. Would they take Alice for a fool? Would they scoff at her slowness? Be harsh and impatient with her?

I thought about the black figure I had seen in the garden, the man who turned his head away from me. Why had he done so? And why should I, of all the family, be singled out to see this phantasmal figure? What did it forbode? Should I see it again?

I had paused, floundering among these thoughts, in my task of repairing the knife-basket, and was sitting like an infant with my knuckles pressed against my brow, waiting for a spasm of acute misery to pass, when my grandmother came to oversee what I was doing.

'Child, child,' she said, sighing, 'you *must* learn to live with that grief. But after a few days, you will see, it will be easier. Now, try to cheer yourself by thinking what new pleasures Alice may be enjoying, what new sights she may be seeing.'

'Yes, ma'am,' I said obediently; though I did not at all agree with her that a few days would amend my grief. (In which I was right and she was wrong.)

I had laid out beside me my brother Robert's old cast-off letter bricks, which, since becoming a scholar at the Grammar School, he, of course, never looked at any more. They were small, but pleasingly carved, with, on one face, the great letter, on the opposite face the small letter, on the third face was a number, and on the fourth a carved figure, as, for example, the Archer for A. Uncle Allen had given them to my brother, but he had never greatly valued them, always preferring outdoor activities.

'Do you know all those letters, Toby?' asked Grandmother Grebell.

'Yes, ma'am.'

'Let me hear you.'

So I went slowly through them, and then she picked out half a dozen at random and asked their names. All my answers were correct; I had known them for the past year.

'Humph,' said my grandmother. 'Do you truly wish to learn to read and write, boy?'

'Oh, *yes*, ma'am. Of course! More than anything else. For then I can write to Alice.'

'But she can't read, child.'

'Surely she will soon learn, with those rich folks.'

My grandmother sighed again. 'Let us hope so . . . But

you, now. It is certainly a pity to let such a spirit go to waste. I will speak again to your father.'

And she went off, muttering to herself, 'After all, James is the richer now by Alice's dowry, poor girl.'

Perhaps it was the thought of the dowry that in the end convinced my father. I think it may also have been my dubious claim to distinction in having seen the Frenchman's ghost, which tale must, in the end, by some route or other, have worked its way round to him; maybe one of the servants told him.—Or, of course, my grandmother. For a day or two I noticed him eyeing me with a kind of perplexity, a kind of irritation; and the conclusion of the matter was that he called me, one day, into his office, and gravely said: 'Toby, your Uncle Allen has offered that you go and learn lessons daily with his godson Hugo Grainger, who will be coming soon to live with him. The chance is too excellent to be let slip, and I have accordingly accepted on your behalf.'

He gave me a somewhat disparaging look, as who should say, why in the world should an opportunity of this value be wasted on such a wretched specimen of humanity?

But I, all amazement, joy, and doubt, hardly dared, or knew, how to respond.

'Well, come: ain't you pleased, boy?' peremptorily demanded my father. 'I understood that to be able to read was your chief ambition? Or so your grandma has it? I thought you would jump for joy.'

His wording was unfortunate. I could see him realising it, just too late.

I said, 'Yes, sir; yes, it is. Oh, sir, is it really so? I am—I *am* very happy. When may I start? Who is this Hugo Grainger?' I had never heard of such a person.

'The lad cannot be here for ten days or so yet; he is at the port of Plymouth. Your uncle will let us know, in due course. Now run along with you; I shall expect you to be twice as diligent and obedient in return for this indulgence—'

But I, with hasty mumbled thanks, made all speed out of my father's presence in case he should suddenly change his mind. Well I knew that I had my grandmother to thank for this; without doubt it was she who had put the notion into Father's head, and very likely into my Uncle Allen's also.

With this bright prospect in store I bore the misery of my sister's loss more patiently. Misery it still was, but at least now I knew that soon I would be able to communicate with her. Dickie Dollinge, our knife-boy, had a cousin, a carter, one Jerrom Bayes, who drove once a week, carrying wine, fish, fleeces, and other such goods as were entrusted to him, as far as Tunbridge Wells; and Dickie told me that if ever I wished to send a message to Alice, Jerrom would be glad to take it for me at a charge of one penny. This knowledge was a great solace and made me all the more eager to be able to write and impart my thoughts and feelings.

In the meantime I asked Grandma Grebell about my Uncle Allen's godson. She knew little enough, but told me what she did.

Uncle Allen, in former years, had bought a part share in a Rye merchant ship, *The Saviour*, and had travelled on various of her voyages, to Madras and Calcutta. In Fort William, at the latter port, he had a partner, Richard Grainger, who had lived out in the Indies for many years. He bought silks and tea there for my uncle and traded in the goods carried out from Europe. Their business prospered, but unluckily my uncle had caught the cholera while in Calcutta, and was like to die of it; he had been shipped back to England, and the lengthy sea-voyage restored him to the indifferent health which had been his lot ever since:

he suffered from pains in his back and legs, sweated profusely at some seasons, had hardly any appetite, and had lost most of his hair. He was obliged to wear a kind of corset when he walked abroad, for, said Dr Wright, his bones were all rotted away. Thus indisposed, he was unable to go voyaging again to the Indies, which grieved him much, for he had been a bold traveller in youth, and said that the lands there, and on the way, were beautiful beyond belief; but he still profited well from the trading voyages of *The Saviour*, and was able to maintain a comfortable establishment for himself and his mother in the house across the street from ours. (Our own house had once been part of the same property, sold by my grandfather to my father on his marriage.)

Uncle Allen was a quiet man. Perhaps because of the long voyages he had undertaken he was of an unsociable habit, preferring his books and silence to the best conversation in the world. He and my father were neither friends nor enemies; they had little in common. I think Uncle Allen was, in his way, devoted to his sister, my mother, and sorry to see her in continual ill health; but, after all, that was the frequent lot of women and there was little that could be done to alleviate it. If he offered her books to read in her chamber she refused them; she, like Alice, was not interested in books.

My grandmother said she knew little about Allen's partner, Richard Grainger, who had left Rye many years ago when a young man, and had remained in India ever since. He had married a lady who went out to join him, and they had a son, but then, last year, both parents had been carried off by the plague and the boy, having no other family, was being sent home to England to be cared for by his godfather.

'How old is he?' I asked my uncle's servant, Abdul

Rahman, meeting him in Market Street, whither I had been sent on an errand.

Abdul counted on his fingers and, with a questioning look, held up eight; he had lived with my uncle so long that he never spoke when silence would serve. Allen had brought him back from India, and I knew that, on the voyage, he had saved my uncle's life by his care and devotion. At the end of it he had been offered the passage money back to his homeland, but preferred to remain where he was greatly valued.

'You met this boy, Abdul? You remember him? Shall I like him?'

Abdul shrugged and made a gesture indicating the will of Heaven. Boys change, his expression conveyed; how could he tell what this one might have become? I would have to wait in patience. And, with the respectful inclination of his head which he offered to all our family, however humble, he went on his speedy and silent way.

Three weeks passed before Hugo arrived. It seemed that a rough passage across the Bay of Biscay had overset his frail health so severely that his life was, at one time, despaired of; that was why he had been put ashore at Plymouth instead of continuing on to Rye in the ship. My uncle went off to meet him and their return was twice delayed.

'It will surely be a new come-out for dot-and-go-one Toby to have a playmate who is sicker still,' remarked my brother Robert with one of his loud laughs. 'For once, Toby, *you* will be able to be the leader.' And he began to mimic the kind of game we would play together, to his own satisfaction.

At first Robert had displayed scant interest in the new scheme (as was his way with anything that did not directly benefit or injure him); but as days went by and it began to be spoken of more, he exhibited a certain resentment.

'Alice goes away to our great cousins in Tunbridge, Toby is to go to Uncle Allen for lessons, what do *I* get?'

'You are the oldest son and, in the fullness of time, will inherit the house and business,' said my father calmly.

'You'll get no dinner unless you take your dirty boots and that tangle of fishing-line out of the back entry,' snapped my grandmother, who displayed no particular fondness at any time for Robert.

On the day when Hugo and Uncle Allen came home, Robert contrived to be lingering in West Street as the coach pulled to a halt, and came to me, sniggering, in the courtyard (where I was mending a pair of my grandmother's clogs) to say, 'Well, I wish you joy of your new playmate, Brother Toby! You might as well strike up a friendship with a piece of string! If he lasts a fortnight, I'm a lowlander!'

And he went whistling on his way down to the Strand to watch a Dutch barge unloading.

I did not like to call at the house uninvited, guessing that the travellers would be very tired. Indeed it was not until the evening of the following day that my grandmother said to me: 'Your uncle says that you may run over to his house after tea and be introduced to your new companion.' When it was time for me to go she said, 'Come here,' and straightened my hair and collar. 'There! Now you look at least like a gentleman's son,' and she sighed.

I had been wondering what I could take as a gift for this new friend. There was Alice's green glass window-eye, which I kept in a secret place, a knot-hole in the wall of the wood-shed, and looked at with wonder and sorrow every time I went there; but this I still regarded as belonging to Alice, it was not mine to give away. During the month of waiting, kind Agnys had bought me, out of her own wage, a little chap-book from a pedlar, in which, following the pictures, I had eagerly puzzled out the words CAT, DOG, BOY, PIE, and so forth. I hated to part with this, but felt it would be the most suitable, indeed the only gift that I could take. For it had occurred to me that, brought up in India, this Hugo might not even be able to speak English. Comforting thought! His education might need to commence even farther back than my own.

I went sidling, shy, and ashamed of my lopsided gait, into the panelled parlour of Uncle Allen's house, where a bright fire burned.

'Here you are, then, Toby, that's right,' said Uncle Allen, in the over-hearty tone used by those who are embarrassed, or unaccustomed to dealing with children. 'And this is Hugo, and now I will leave you two to become better acquainted. Mr Ellis from Playden is going to be your tutor, but, as Hugo is still very knocked-up from the journey, you may have one or two days more of idleness; Mr Ellis will not commence his duties until next Monday.'

And Uncle Allen walked quickly out of the room.

'Hallo,' I said, finding my voice with a croak.

'Hallo,' quietly responded the boy who lay in the armchair.

His feet were propped on a stool and he was swathed in shawls. Even so I could see that, for his age, he was tall and pitifully thin—thinner even than I. His skin was pale as pearl, but topped with a thatch of the most amazing yellow hair. It fairly blazed in the dim room, like that of some angelic messenger in a stained-glass window. What colour his eyes were I could not, at that time, see, but later discovered them to be a pale, intelligent grey.

'I brought you a gift,' I said, and awkwardly handed him the little book. He took it and turned the pages carefully and politely. But while he did so I noticed that the chair in which he lay, and the low table beside him, were crammed and piled with books; one, which he had evidently laid aside as I entered lay face-down on his lap. And there was ink, and a pen, and notebooks filled with writing . . .

Hot blood seems to come up from my toes, and to flood my face, my hair, my neck, every part of me.

This boy, only a couple of years older than myself (he was nine, I later discovered) was already reading, not children's picture-books or spelling primers, but books that even I could tell were written for adults.

'I—I am sorry, Hugo,' I gulped out foolishly. 'I made a mistake. I was stupid. I thought that—like me—you had never learned to read. Give me back the book.'

I stood by him quivering, wishing myself under the ground, thinking how loudly and raucously my brother Robert would laugh, later, when he heard of this.

Hugo held the little book between his hands, and looked at me over the top of it. He said: 'How could you tell? It was a very kind thought to bring me this. For all you knew, I might speak only Pushtu or Tamil.'

'What are those?

'Languages they speak in India.'

'You know so *much* that I do not!'

'Listen, Toby,' said Hugo. 'About England I have everything to learn. Do you think I have not been frightened on the journey here, wondering what sort of people I was coming amongst, wondering if they would laugh at me for my sickly colour, or my ignorance of your ways? But when you came to see me you bring me a present, you—' he sought for a word—'you are honest with me about what you feel, you do not try to put me down. I can tell by your face, Toby Lamb, that you are a kind person, you don't give yourself airs, or try to make other people feel uncomfortable.'

'Give myself airs! I should think not!'

'Sit down,' said Hugo. 'Pull that other stool over.'

I did as he suggested, sticking out my lame leg awkwardly.

'Uncle Allen told me that you are lame,' said Hugo. 'That is very hard luck. But listen—Abdul is going to rub me, three times a day, with some medicine he makes himself, Thorn Oil, for my joints are very weak and I have rheumatic pains from a fever I caught when I was younger. Uncle Allen derives great benefit from this oil. Why should Abdul not rub your lame leg also? Perhaps that might strengthen it, make it less lame.'

'I've always had it,' I said helplessly. Already I was becoming infected by Hugo's enthusiasm, his wish to effect an improvement in any matter that was amiss, to change all that might be wrong and put it right as fast as possible, to make the world, as far as he could see it, a better place.

'Just because you have always had it need not mean that you always will; need it?' said Hugo reasonably.

'I don't know!'

'Well, I shall ask Uncle Allen. I am obliged to do exercises, also, every day—they were taught me by an Indian doctor, a kind of priest—to strengthen my weak arms and legs and back. I shall teach them to you and we can do them together. Because I want to go out as soon as I can and see this place—the town—it seems very beautiful. Is it not?'

'Oh, it is!' I assured him. 'Rye is the finest town in Sussex. There is the tower—and the walls—and the gates—and the guns—and the ships—'

'And that huge marsh that we passed over, I want to see that, and the shore. Is it far away?'

Too far, I had always thought. My brother and his friends made nothing of running off to Camber, or Winchelsea Strand, but for me it was a long, lonely, painful distance. But with a companion, the distance would seem less . . .

'Not so very far,' I said. 'There are beautiful shells, cowries and goldshells—'

Then I fell silent, remembering the Indian shells that Uncle Allen had brought home, a hundred times bigger and more gorgeous than any found on our chilly beaches.

'I want to see it all,' he said. 'And you will explain everything, and I shall tell you about India. By and by! We have plenty of time. Now, do you want to learn to read?'

'Of course,' I stammered.

'Well, then, look here.' He dug down under some larger books and produced a little old well-worn one. 'I have had this since I was four,' he said, handling it fondly. 'Mamma gave it to me.' And he began reading aloud to me out of it, the story of Fortunatus and the Wishing-Cap, pointing out the words to me as he did so. By the time he had got to Little Jack Horner I was breathlessly echoing the words as he read, and sometimes anticipating him. 'There! You see, you can read already,' said he. 'In a week you will be writing as well.'

'Oh, that is what I really want! So that I can write to Alice!'

'Alice, who is Alice?'

I poured out to Hugo the tale of how she had been sent away, and how miserably I missed her.

'And you want to write to her?' said Hugo. 'Why, there is nothing simpler. Tell me what you wish to say, and I will put it down for you.'

'Would you? Truly?'

'Why in the world not? Here—' he pulled the inkstand towards him, and trimmed a pen. 'Only tell me what you wish to say. How do you begin? "My dear Alice—"?'

'My dearest Alice . . .' Without my having to think

about it at all, the letter came flowing out of me. 'I miss you, every minute of every day. And every night as well. How do you fare? Grandmother says that in a family such as ours, illness and good health must shift about from one person to another. There is a balance that must be kept between such things, as between success and failure. So, if I am down, you must be up, and I hope this is so, dearest Alice, for I would gladly pass weeks of unhappiness if it meant that fortune smiled on you. I think that our mother misses you greatly, she has taken to her bed. Uncle Allen's godson has come from India to live in Rye, he is called Hugo and is kindly writing this letter for me. Now I shall be able to send a letter to you every week, and soon I shall write it in my own hand, for Uncle Allen is to have me taught reading and lessons by Mr Ellis, and Hugo too. No more now from your loving brother Toby.'

Hugo was just sprinkling sand on the letter to dry it when Uncle Allen walked in.

'Toby has tired you long enough for today, my boy,' he said to Hugo. 'But I can see that you two are going to be famous friends.' A quick smile lit his rather gloomy countenance. 'However you must be off now, Toby.'

'Oh, yes, uncle. I—I hope I have not tired you too greatly,' I said to Hugo and, to my uncle, 'At what hour shall I come in the morning?'

'You can't wait to be back, eh?' He smiled again. 'Shall we say nine o'clock?'

'Here, Toby.' Hugo passed me the little book of stories. 'An exchange! See if you can read the one about Jack and the Beanstalk.'

I read it to myself in bed, and was soundly beaten by my father who, going up to bed, glimpsed my rushlight burning. I was in dread that he would forbid tomorrow's visit, but he only punished me by a breakfast of dry bread;

to instil in me the values of thrift and economy, he said.

'How does it advantage me to have you taught reading if you then use the hours of darkness wasting my candles?'

After he left me the night before I had lain awake in a sweat of worry, wondering (for I had already given the folded letter to Jerrom Bayes, and he had promised to see that it was given into Alice's own hand) *who* would read the letter aloud to her? Would it be my cousin Honoria, in her weary, sardonic voice? Or Captain Wakehurst, whose tones held at all times a kind of sneer? I did not like to think of my letter coming under their scrutiny.

But perhaps there would be some kind person in that household, like Polly, like Agnys, who would read the letter in a friendly and sympathetic manner. Most devoutly I hoped so.

Hugo had provided the penny. He had plenty of money, he said, for his father had been a wealthy man. It was in trust for him till he should reach the age of twenty-one, but Uncle Allen gave him a comfortable allowance. I could pay back the penny when I was a famous man of letters, he said.

After my breakfast of dry bread I went across the road to Uncle Allen's house, and Hugo and I talked until past noon. He told me about his life in Calcutta and the journey over on *The Saviour*. And I told him about Rye, and how both my father and Uncle Allen had been Mayor at different times, and so had my grandfather and great-grandfather, and about our brewery, and how the King had once passed three nights in our house. Naturally Hugo was very interested in the King.

'Was he very handsome? Did he wear a crown?'

'No, he was very fat, and wore a wig. And he spoke only German; none of us could comprehend a word he said. And his servants spoke German too.'

'How queer,' said Hugo thoughtfully, 'how queer to

have a foreign king. But I suppose it is often so. Once, after all, the king of this land was Julius Caesar.'

'Julius Caesar? Who was he?'

If I had had any notion, at the start of our friendship, how immensely much more knowledge Hugo possessed than I, I would never have dared approach him in the first place. I would have crept away, devoured by shame, to hide my head in some shed or stable. For already, at the age of nine, he knew Latin, Greek, and French; he had long ago finished with grammar and read these languages as easily as his mother tongue. Fortunately, by the time I realised the extent of the educational gap between us, we were fast friends, and the gap was of no consequence. In two days he had taught me to read, and, if he thought it singular that a lad of my age, the son of a man who was Mayor and a well-respected merchant of the town, had received so little schooling, he, with his usual sensitivity and kindliness, made no comment upon the matter, but quietly set about doing his utmost to lessen the gulf between our attainments.

In a few ways, I was his equal. When Mr Ellis (a grave, friendly young curate) began teaching us, it was discovered that I had a natural aptitude for Euclid and mathematical subjects, in which Hugo was somewhat deficient, for his parents, who had taught him all else, were no mathematicians. So I became less inclined to fear that I was naturally, incurably stupid, and indeed Mr Ellis was able to give good reports of my progress to my father. My speed in acquiring knowledge was, in part, due to my fervent wish to catch up with Hugo, and, in larger part, to Hugo's own kindly assistance and coaching.

During the first winter we spent together the weather was very bad; rain or snow fell almost every day and gales lashed the town; from my attic window I could see nothing but black clouds over Romney Marsh and the ships' masts dancing crazily down by the dockside; for a long time it was thought inadvisable for Hugo to set foot out of doors. Therefore we spent months of happy days together indoors while Hugo read me stories about Ulysses and Hercules and the siege of Troy and the battle of Salamis. And I began to tackle Latin and Greek (French I already knew a little from talking to Gilles Flory, a Frenchman who worked in the brewery) and we both laboured at drawing, in which subject neither of us excelled. When tired of our books we played chess or cribbage or marbles or dominoes, or simply talked.

Hugo, for a start, wished to hear all about my family. Due to one cause or another, he had met none of them yet; my father was too occupied with business to visit a sickly boy who was no kin of his, my mother too unwell; Robert was not interested, the small ones were not invited, for it was thought that Hugo would find them too fatiguing. Grandmother Grebell, of course, he saw constantly, and she treated him with the same impatient, perceptive kindness that she gave all of us.

The person that Hugo really wished to hear about was Alice. He asked me endless questions about her.

'It is so strange and hard that, just as I came, she should have gone,' he would sometimes observe, in a melancholy tone.

My possession of Alice, in heart, in memory, was the one treasure, I sometimes thought, that righted the unequal balance between me and Hugo; he had learning, skill at languages, a sweet nature; but *I* had a dear sister, and that he did greatly envy. He had, he said, met no girls at all in Calcutta where he had been brought up. To have a sister, a beloved sister, as familiar as a friend, and yet so different—what a joy that must be! He never tired of hearing me tell about her.

And he was unfailingly willing, always ready to indite

a letter to her at my dictation, and would discuss things to tell her, and the best way of putting down what I had to say. 'Hugo suggests—' 'Hugo reminds me to tell you—' became familiar phrases. And yet—I sound selfish to myself but I must say this—although I appreciated Hugo's help, I did not altogether like sharing my letters to Alice in this way, and made as much haste as I could in learning, so as to hasten the day when I could perform this office for myself. This, of course, it was a matter of pride to do as soon as I could string two words together. I blushed with shame, later, to think of those ill-written, ill-spelt missives that first went off by the hand of Jerrom Bayes.

Jerrom, a dusty, red-faced, laconic individual swore to me that he was able to deliver the letters to Alice in person.

'For they lives in a new house on the edge o' town,' he explained. 'Hazelwood House, 'tis called, a grand new place with a deal o' wrought-iron fencework, and a shrubbery, and a garden grotto. Mistress Alice, she do oftways walk in the shrubbery and 'tis only to hand the letter over the fence.'

'She is always alone? Never anybody with her?'

'Nay, she be always by her lone. Though,' he added, 'there mought be someone a-setting in the summerhouse. In there I can't see.'

Alice's situation sounded sad to me, and I discussed it with Hugo.

'But perhaps,' he said, 'she likes to be on her own for part of the day. She has come from a big family where she was always busy and in company. Perhaps she finds privacy a treat.'

He spoke kindly to reassure me, but I did not wholly believe him.

And, as the months wore on, I became more and more

troubled by the fact that, though I faithfully adhered to my promise of writing to Alice every week, not a letter, not one single letter, did I ever receive in return.

'Well: perhaps she has found no one to teach her to write,' said Hugo. 'Though it is singular, I must say, if they are such great rich folk; you'd think they'd feel shame not to have her taught.'

'Or she could at least dictate a letter to someone,' I worried.

I asked my grandmother about it.

'Toby,' she said, 'it's no use troubling your head. Alice may have new interests, new occupations. Very likely she has no time for writing letters. Or does not care to be reminded of her former life. Or her new friends may not choose that she should write to you. My best advice to you is to forget her. You have your own new friend, and your new pursuits. Try to forget her,' she repeated.

But I knew I could not do that. I said stubbornly: 'When I am older I shall travel to Tunbridge Wells and see for myself how she does with those grand folk.'

Grandmother Grebell shook her head.

'You can't do that, Toby. Not unless they invited you. It would not be seemly.'

Nonetheless, this visit to Tunbridge Wells became a secret plan between me and Hugo. Just as soon as we were older and in better health . . .

A programme of measures to improve Hugo's health (and mine also) was, by us both, meanwhile most diligently and unremittingly sustained. Twice every day Abdul Rahman strenuously rubbed Hugo's limbs and back with his preparation of Thorn Oil, and, since Hugo was eloquent in praise of its remedial effects, I too was permitted to undergo this treatment, and did begin to feel, after two or three months, that the muscles in my dangling, crippled leg appeared to be enlarging and becoming more responsive to my wishes. My limp, I thought hopefully, was not quite so severe; and I believed that I was able to hold myself more upright.

I had, of course, told Hugo the tale of old Mrs Tubsey and how nearly she had ended my life before it had well begun. 'Indeed many times I have wished that she had done so.'

'Then your wish was wicked and senseless,' said Hugo forcefully. 'How can you possibly tell, at this present, what you may do later with your life? How can you tell what hidden happiness lies in store for you?'

'I shall never be a father, for one thing,' said I. (For that was another of the ill results of Mrs Tubsey's negligence.) 'Not that I care so much for that. Who wants a pack of noisy disobedient brats? In any case, when I am a man, I do not intend to marry; I shall seek out Alice and we shall live together in Look-Out Cottage. So she always promised me.'

'No, no,' said Hugo teasingly. '*I* am going to marry Alice. And then we shall all three live happily together in Look-Out Cottage.—Where is Look-Out Cottage, by the way?'

Look-Out Cottage, I told him, was a dwelling that had once greatly taken my fancy when Grandmother Grebell permitted me to accompany her on one of her rare excursions to visit an old widowed friend in the neighbour town of Winchelsea. It was a tiny house that, tucked on the hillside behind the Strand Gate, commanded a handsome view of the marsh, the sea with fitfully glancing sunbeams, and Rye, like a coronet of red brick perched on its knoll two miles away.

Look-Out Cottage was one of the first places I had promised to show Hugo as soon as we were both able to walk as far as two miles.

'In any case,' continued Hugo, 'even if you are unable

to father a family, you can make a great name for yourself, you can make yourself some memorial that will live after you. There are so many ways in which a man may become famous—write books, go into Parliament and pass new laws, or heal people, or invent machines, like Leonardo da Vinci. (And *he* had no children—or not that we hear about. Nor did Queen Elizabeth.) Isn't it queer, Toby, how our lives are affected, all the time, every minute of the day, by people long since dead, old kings, or law-makers, or religious leaders—even by common people, of whom we have never heard?'

'Yes, that is certainly true,' said I, slowly, reflecting over what he had said. And then I gave a sudden shiver, recalling (what, so far, I had never told Hugo) the apparition that I had seen in the garden behind Lamb House, that silent, mysterious figure from the cobwebby past of Rye. Why, I asked myself, as I had so many times before, why had it been given to *me* to witness that phantom? What message had it for *me*, that was intended for no other person? 'Perhaps ghosts,' I went on ponderingly, 'perhaps ghosts are the image left behind by unhappy people who have left no other memorial—who want to be remembered somehow, even if it is only the memory of their pain that is passed on?'

He laughed and said, 'If that is so, Toby, perhaps you and I are nothing but the raw material of a ghost story.' Then, growing more serious, he added, '*I* am going to make a great name for myself, I swear it.'

We were at the time performing the exercises that the Buddhist monk had taught Hugo, and that he had painstakingly passed on to me; we worked at them most assiduously for an hour every day. The first portion consisted of balance, which looked, I daresay, very ludicrous if there had been any onlooker, but, the teacher had insisted and Hugo affirmed, was of sovereign importance both for mental tranquillity and physical wellbeing.

'Animals and birds have a complete sense of balance, they never trip and fall, they are never unprepared,' said Hugo. 'When did you ever see a cat fall over?'

And so, at the commencement of our exercise hour, we both stood on one leg for five minutes, clasping the raised ankle with the hand on that side, the other hand uplifted, pointing to the sky.

My brother Rob, chancing to peer through the window one day while we were performing this exercise, burst into such a fit of laughter that he fell down in West Street, and I was not to hear the last of his teasing for many months.

'Oh, what fun! The two one-legged cripples! Oh, my eye! Don't I just wish the rest of my mates had been there to see you!'

To my joy, I had found that Hugo's promise of greater mental equilibrium accompanying better bodily balance was quite valid; my brother's taunts troubled me far less than they would have done a year ago.

Untroubled, I replied, 'I'll wager that I can stand on one leg longer than you can, Rob.'

'Who *wants* to stand on one leg?' And Rob ran off to play football by the Tillingham River.

'Well,' remarked Hugo when I told him of this exchange, 'I daresay we do look very comical—like two storks standing side by side.'

Rob was filled with a mixture of envy and scorn by my friendship with Hugo, from which he was so wholly excluded. 'What do you *do*, in there, all day?' he demanded.

'Learn our lessons with Mr Ellis. Talk. Read books.'

'*Books!* Faugh!'

Just the same, curiosity gnawed at Robert and, after some months, he said, 'Why don't *I* come and talk to Hugo? Wouldn't he like to see somebody other than you, Toby, all day and every day? I lay I could teach him plenty of new games and pastimes you have never thought to mention.'

I was not enthusiastic about this suggestion and delayed proposing it to Hugo, but Rob's pestering me, day after day, 'Have you asked him yet? What does he say?' at last induced me to report his wish to Hugo, who said, 'Why, of course. Let him come whenever he likes. But Robert on his own, if you please! I am not anxious to meet half a dozen of his friends as well.' For he had seen them run past the window in West Street, kicking, tripping, and jostling one another. 'Nor would Uncle Allen wish it,' he added.

Uncle Allen's house was always kept exquisitely neat, with his shells, engravings, glassware from Venice, Indian carvings, all carefully dusted and in their places.

So Rob came, half swaggering, half abashed, and Hugo received him politely. But the visit was not a success; they had nothing to say to one another, and, greatly to my relief, it was never repeated. Rob voted my friend 'a sad dull stick' and Hugo said reflectively, 'It is wonderful that two brothers can be so different.'

'Alice is different from either of us.'

'Ah—Alice. Well, she would be different, of course. Yet from many of the things you tell me about her, Toby, I would guess that you and she resemble one another in many ways.'

'Not in appearance!' I said laughing. 'Alice is so pleasing to look at—like a soft little dark-plumaged bird, with a robin's bright eye.'

I had tried to draw pictures of her sometimes for Hugo, but it was useless; I never acquired the needful skill. But after some months my own looks, to my secret joy and amazement, were beginning slowly to change. Whether because of Abdul Rahman's rubbing with Thorn Oil, or the exercises, or my happier circumstances, I had grown somewhat in height, and ate with better appetite (this was partly to encourage Hugo, who picked no more than a sparrow when he first arrived) and latterly, when I went in to visit my poor mother, these days entirely confined to her bed, I was quite startled to encounter my own image in her mirror. Also my lame leg was not quite so lame.

'You look better, Toby,' Mother sometimes faintly said. 'You are fleshing out a little—your hair has more life in it—your skin a better colour—that gladdens me—'

'Oh, ma'am—Mother—if only we could hear from Alice—if only we knew how *she* was faring—'

But she would sigh and say nothing.

One day, though, she did say to me, 'I have heard from your Cousin Honoria.'

'Is Alice well?' I demanded. 'What does our cousin say?'

'Alice is well, they have bought her new clothes. Cousin Honoria reports that she makes herself useful about the house, conducts herself dutiful and submissive as she ought—'

'Will they come to Rye? May we not see Alice?'

'No. Cousin Honoria believes that not advisable. Lest the girl, after settling down, be troubled by a wish for her own home.'

I felt as if my heart were being violently squeezed, like an apple in a cider-press. If they had so little confidence as that in Alice's happiness—

'Oh, ma'am! May she not come home again? I think—I feel—I am sure that she is not happy there with them. Why, why does she never answer any of my letters?'

'No, Toby,' came the weary voice. 'Matters may not be altered now. They are best left as they are ... And, respecting your correspondence, Cousin Honoria thinks it best you discontinue writing to your sister; your letters, she says, only give pain and stir up old recollections.'

'I am not to write to her?'

'Not so often, at least. Once every two or three months, perhaps—'

'But that is cruel! Very cruel.' And I repeated, 'I am sure

she is not happy. I have dreadful dreams about her at night. Last night I dreamed that a snake was in her chamber—a huge snake, that crept its way out of her bureau drawer—'

'Be quiet, Toby!' almost shrieked my mother, pressing her hands against her ears. 'I will not listen! I do not wish to hear! Leave me! Send Agnys—' And I heard her desolate voice murmur, as I crept away from the bedside, '*I* dream about her too.'

Paying no heed to the Wakehursts' prohibition, I continued to write my letters to Alice. Poor Alice, I thought. Why can she only come to us in dreams? Why has she no other means of expressing her wishes? The least I can do is keep her in touch with what happens here. So I wrote about my lessons, about Hugo, about the exercises that we did, about Father, these days more than ever involved in public duties, about Sophy and Moses, who, from a pair of angelic little cherubs, were now grown into a pair of very ordinary, noisy, ill-behaved children. My grandmother, ageing now, and much occupied about my mother's sick-chamber, had less energy and time to spare for them than she had had for Rob, Alice, and me, so they had become somewhat out-of-hand. Father, after considering and perhaps luckily rejecting Hawney's Charity School, had entered them at a little day school presided over by an old lady, the Widow Julians, who had formerly been wife to one of the jurats of Rye; to eke out her scanty funds she entertained in her home (a tiny cottage perched on the cliff at the end of Baddings Lane) a dozen or so children at a time, and taught them what she knew, which seemed but little, judging from her results with Moses and Sophy. It was my task to take or bring them to her establishment, and if I asked what they had done during the day, Sophy would cry, 'Oh, Moses was top-of-the-stairs today, and I was second!' It seemed that their place on the stair demonstrated their position in class. The higher steps were the best, Moses said, because from there you could see out of the window and over to the river.

'Why,' demanded Hugo of me in his usual calm and pondering way, 'Why does your father send these little ones to school at the ages of five and three when he never sent you at all?'

'Oh—because, because, I suppose, I had always made myself rather useful at home, dipping rushlights and so forth, whereas Sophy and Moses do nothing but plague the life out of the servants and my grandmother; also because my father never expected me to live beyond the age of seven or so, therefore he begrudged the expenditure of money on me. It was a lucky hour for me, Hugo, when you came to live with Uncle Allen.'

I did not mention the ghost in the garden. That spectral encounter had also, perceptibly, altered my father's attitude towards me, though he never spoke of it to me, nor I to him. But James Lamb was an intensely practical man: 'Every single thing in this world', I have countless times heard him say, 'has its use and can be turned to advantage.' I have no doubt whatsoever that he believed the ghost played its part and must be of some, as yet unrevealed importance; therefore I, as its witness, must also somewhere have my value. I believed this myself; though I had not seen the spectre a second time I used to stroll, sometimes, at dusk, in the tiny walled garden, or in the grass-bordered alley that led to it and the brewery—hoping, perhaps, for another visitation, or just for confirmation of what I had seen before. But none came. And I still (for reasons obscure to myself) had never related this experience to Hugo. Oh, if only I had done so! What trouble that might have spared us.

I kept the ghost to myself; it was the only secret I had from Hugo.

A winter, a summer, and another winter passed before

it was judged advisable for Hugo to set foot out of doors. By that time he was heartily sick of confinement in Uncle Allen's house, despite all its treasures, and prayed Dr Wright not to keep him immured any longer. And, a warm spring coming in with the year 1729, bringing daffodils in February and apple blossoms in April, the doctor at last gave his permission.

My relation with Dr Wright, in all this long time of Hugo's incarceration, had been, on the one side, from me toward him, of apprehensive respect (for Dr Wright was an irascible man, not slow to speak his mind, and decidedly no friend to my father); and on his side, towards me, a species of amazed disapproval, not unmixed with hot-tempered kindliness. For, firstly, he said, I had no right to be alive in this world at all, considering the circumstances of my arrival into it (not the least important of which had been Dr Wright's own exclusion from the business, due, as I have mentioned, to my father's parsimony). And then secondly, said Dr Wright, it was clean against Nature for Hugo and me, but particularly myself, to be improving in health, as we visibly were, and thriving, not from his regime (for Uncle Allen retained him merely to watch over Hugo and advise in case of serious problems, which, mercifully, were lacking) but from the ministrations of what he termed a heathen Mohammedan. This was what chiefly stuck in Dr Wright's craw, and had he not been a man of high intelligence and probity, he might have denied the evidence of his own senses. But that he did not do. He and my uncle were excellent friends (taking into account their diverging opinions and misanthropic natures) and would argue, sometimes, for an hour together.

So it was only after the carefully considered permission of Dr Wright that I escorted Hugo, first across the street to visit Lamb House, and then, by inching and careful stages, round the town of Rye.

Lamb House delighted him. So warm! he said, so spacious! with its friendly panelled rooms, its wide shallow handsome stair, and the atmosphere it breathed of comfort and company, of being a family home, with children scurrying up the back stairs and down the front (which they were not supposed to do), of the maids baking and chattering over their household tasks in kitchen and offices; of my father hard at work engaged on some weighty business of the town in his study; of the menservants in the yard, chopping wood, drawing water, or tending to the horses.—There was also, it was true, my mother, silent in her chamber; I led Hugo, tiptoeing, to visit her, but it was one of her bad days, she lay there looking like a wax image of herself and only raised her eyelids long enough to murmur—'Hugo . . . Ah yes . . . Allen's ward . . .' before making the faint gesture with her wrist which indicated that she had not strength for us any longer.

'*Oh Toby!*' breathed Hugo in horror as we returned down the stairs. 'She is so like you—she is the image of you—you never said that!'

'She is more like Alice,' I whispered.

When Hugo had been led all over the house, from the four skylit attics to the brick vaulted cellar, he said he thought it was the happiest place he had ever been in; it seemed to hum with goodwill to all who entered the door. I told him this was because he had been shut up for so long in one room; he would need to see more houses before he could judge fairly. 'Well, I will see more, but I am sure this one will always be the best,' he said. 'It seems to open its heart to you as you step inside. If it were mine, I would never leave it.'

Perhaps, I thought, the house felt so because my father had built it as a gift for my mother, five years after they were married. Perhaps the walls and windows and stairways echoed back some of the love and hope that had gone into their building. But I did not say this. The contrast with their present condition was too sad.—Not that my father did not still love my mother. I am sure that, in his own silent way, he did so. But matters had turned out far otherwise than he had hoped.

Robert came clattering in with some of his mates, and Hugo and I beat a swift retreat to the garden. I offered to show him over the brewery (though my father did not encourage us children to go in there, unless sent on a specific errand) but the hot smell of malt and hops, the pungent yeasty steam and great splashes of foam repelled him; he still had a delicate, queasy stomach and was easily offended by strong and coarse odours; so we turned along the little garden-lane that led down into Mermaid Street.

I did not mention the ghost.

Of course I thought about it. As we passed the spot I could so easily have remarked, 'Oh, by the way, Hugo, on this spot I once saw a spectre.' But somehow my tongue clove to the roof of my mouth and I remained silent.

In Mermaid Street I said, 'We had better not go down this steep street, Hugo. Should you not return home now?' but he was not ready to go inside yet, he would go farther, so we turned uphill, round the corner, past Uncle Allen's house and on into Church Square, past the Customs Office. We walked to the Tower, and looked down from the Gun Gardens, where the great guns point their muzzles towards anybody who might come marauding from the French coast, and over the harbour to the sea. The world shone like an opened shell.

'Another day we will go over there, to the shore,' said Hugo, filling his lungs with the salty air. 'Now I have come out, I am going to go *everywhere*. And you are going with me, Toby!'

So, in the end, we did. But firstly, together, we explored Rye, and I showed him all the crannies, the alleys, the look-out points, the secret stairways down the cliff, the wharfs, the dockside, the market place, the old monastery, the lower Gun Gardens—all the places in which, formerly, I had felt sorrowful and solitary, because I had no one with whom to enjoy them. Alice, though dear, was too old, and busy with her tasks in the house. But now it seemed sometimes as if Hugo and I were the sole inhabitants of the town, as if it had no other citizens; we roamed and rambled in an enclosed private world, a bubble of our own exclusive companionship. Nobody knew Hugo; and if they looked at me it was in a fleeting, perplexed manner, as if to say, 'Who can that be? It has a look of young Toby Lamb, to be sure, but it cannot be he—Toby Lamb is a poor cripple, but that boy seems to walk well enough . . .' We were so happy, wandering around Rye, our lot seemed so removed from that of common mortals, that I once said to Hugo, 'We are like two ghosts, nobody can see us.' 'Perhaps we are ghosts,' he fancifully returned. 'Perhaps we are not here *now*, but will be in one hundred, two hundred years.' 'Oh, why stop there? Why not make it three hundred, four hundred?' I laughed.

'Will Rye still be here in four hundred years?'

'Why not? It has been here more than seven hundred already. Edward the Confessor gave it to the monks of Fécamp. You and I, Hugo, are just grains of dust in the history of Rye.'

'Gave it to the monks at Fécamp? Was it his to give? What a queer act, to give away a town? I must read about that in the history books when we return home.'

So we wandered, so we talked.

That autumn my father said to me, 'Toby, you and Hugo seem so much better now, so much more as—' he hesitated—'as boys of your age should be—I am debating

with myself whether you should not now enrol as students at Peacock's School, like your brother. Or you, at all events—I cannot legislate for your uncle Allen's godson.'

I gaped at my father, aghast.

'Go to the Grammar School? Stop taking our lessons with Mr Ellis?'

'You should learn to accommodate yourself to other boys,' my father returned firmly. 'You and Hugo are too much off on your own together. After all, later on, it is my purpose to induct you into the brewing trade—'

I mumbled something about my brother Robert. After all, it was he who would inherit the business. He was the eldest son.

'I know, I know,' said my father testily. 'But there is room for you both. It is an expanding market, with this new porter that the lower orders have taken to drinking so plentifully. And I hear on good authority that Government will soon take steps to limit the atrocious gin trade, so our business will flourish even better. But—' he coughed and looked at me sidelong. 'Your brother Robert has no great aptitude for commerce. He will deal well enough with the men, he has the gift for that—' Father came to a halt, and I felt a little sorry for him. Robert was a dolt, and would never be anything more than a dolt. My grandmother had been right in her judgment. It would go hard with Father, if all his carefully tended brewing business were to be thrown into disorder by Robert's stupidity and lack of interest.

With a certain sad irony I wondered if it had ever occurred to my father to wish that he could appoint me his heir instead of Robert. But of course he could not, because of my disability.—In any case, there were still Moses and little Jem to fall back on.

I did not in the least wish to enter the Grammar School at this point, but judged it prudent to make no protest at

that moment. For Father was an obstinate man, and any opposition only strengthened his resolution.

I did, however, enter a vehement plea with Uncle Allen that he would intercede on my behalf, that he would argue for a continuance of the present state of affairs.

This he most readily did.

'It would be the greatest piece of folly in the world, James, to shift the boys at this juncture,' he told my father roundly. 'We have excellent reports of them from Ellis, they are well disposed and studious at their books, and Toby, who was so far behind in all his studies, bids fair to catch up with Hugo. Not only that, but Ellis informs me that both are so far ahead of lads of comparable age at Peacock's that such a transfer would only hamper and disadvantage them.'

'But they never mix with their fellows,' said my father.

'And so? What harm in that? *I* never mix with my fellows and see no occasion to,' said Uncle Allen. 'My fellows in Rye are a set of boorish louts, who are of no conceivable interest to me. And here's Ellis saying that the boys will in a few years be ready to enter Cambridge; he suggests Jesus College, where he himself matriculated; or I've a notion that Toby would distinguish himself at Gray's Inn where I got my learning—'

'*University?*' said my father, as shocked as if Uncle Allen had suggested we should travel to the Bermudas and learn shark-fishing.

'Why not? Others have done so.'

Still my father argued and demurred. He did not see the point of such prolonged education. For what did it fit a man? Here Uncle Allen patiently pointed out to him that, in any case, if it had not been for our association together, both Hugo and I would probably have been dead long since. (I did not hear this conversation myself,

but Hugo, who did, faithfully reported it to me.)

'It seems to me,' said Allen, 'that these boys were, in some sort, meant to be companions, and should not now be separated. Which, I assure you, they would be, for I have not the slightest intention of sending Hugo to Peacock's—an excellent school of its kind, I don't doubt, for boys of the robuster sort, but not appropriate, at this time, for Hugo. Nor, I should have thought, for Toby. Of course, if you feel you cannot afford to continue with Ellis's fee—I shall be glad to defray—'

This pinked my father, whose business was, in fact, expanding handsomely, and he hastily told Allen to think no more of the suggestion, so long as the boys were satisfying Ellis's requirements, let that be an end to the matter.

Hugo and I breathed again. Cambridge—or Gray's Inn—seemed a long way off, and in the meantime we had our freedom and our kindly tutor.

'And whether Cambridge or Gray's Inn,' said Hugo, 'we shall be there together.'

'That's of course.'

The following spring, the year 1730, when I was eleven and Hugo thirteen, Uncle Allen developed an interest in the study of wild plants. Botany, he said, had always been a favourite pursuit of the ancients, and we would do well to emulate them; in the science of wild plants might be found all manner of useful and life-saving information. Why, he told us, even the common sow-thistle was, by Pliny, accounted a very wholesome and nourishing article of diet; Pliny related how Theseus, prior to his encounter with the bull that was ravaging the plain of Marathon, took as a prelude and appropriate nourishment a large dish of sow-thistle.

'Well, let us by all means follow the example of Theseus,' says Hugo cheerfully. 'Only tell us, Uncle

Allen, where sow-thistle is to be found, and we will fetch you all you can eat of it.'

Allen took him with perfect seriousness and, to promote this study, purchased for us a little old pony trap, a kind of gig, so that we might venture farther afield and obtain for him specimens of various plants. (He did not extend his botanical studies to going out into the countryside himself.) Our aged and humble conveyance was to us a source of wonderful enjoyment; in it (when our lessons were done and Mr Ellis satisfied) we adventured all over the marsh, to New Romney and Lydd and Brookland, or inland, to Appledore and Tenterden and Bodiam, or down to the shore at Winchelsea and Camber, and we brought back to Uncle Allen great stores of plants and roots, not to mention sea-shells and samphire and sea-slugs and other slimy things from the strand, all of which Uncle Allen carefully listed and catalogued. Often, out on the marsh, the track would come to a stop, for the marsh is all seamed with sluices and dykes, tide-gates and water-lets; and we must continue on foot, splashing through channels or over single plank bridges; but there was never the least anxiety about leaving our trap, for Fanny, the little old mule who drew it, was the laziest beast in creation and would stand happily on one spot for hours together; we always provided ourselves with pockets full of coarse brown sugarknobs, begged from Agnys, which were required to persuade Fanny into motion again, once she had sunk into a doze.

The marsh was an unfailing source of plants—we found orchises and water-lilies, kingcups and flowering rush and fritillaries, and disturbed great flocks of waterbirds, moorhens, curlews, great grey herons, swans, who hissed at us ferociously when we approached their nests, and hundreds of different species of ducks.

The marsh was exciting and mysterious; but the woodlands were our greatest delight.

I can remember one of our earliest excursions, when, leaving Fanny tethered to a stile, we wandered into some woods near Udimore. It was April—the hazels were budding, the birds in full chorus, and the ground carpeted as far as the eye could see with blue. It was not a mere pale sky colour, but dark, intense, luminous, almost seeming to vibrate in the air. And the scent was all about us too—a cool fragrance, like that of cucumber.

'Great heavens,' says Hugo, looking about him. 'What are these?'

'Wild hyacinths. Bluebells.'

'I never saw such a mass of colour in my life before! It seems wrong to walk on them. And yet how are we to make our way into the wood otherwise?'

We picked our path as best we could, inevitably crushing hundreds of flowers under our feet—yet there were so many that perhaps it did not matter.

'I wonder why nature is so lavish in some ways and so skinflint in others?' said Hugo. 'Why so many bluebells, when there are only one each of you and I?'

'In the view of Nature, I daresay you and I strongly resemble all the other boys in Rye!'

'What are those birds, all making such a loud noise?'

'Nightingales.'

The wood was full of them, buzzing and gargling.

'Is *that* what a nightingale sounds like? I have read so many poems about them. I always supposed that it was a gentle, melodious song, heard only at night.'

'Well,' I said, 'I suppose they are enjoying the warm sun, like us.'

Agnys had put us up a picnic of cold chicken legs and apple tarts—the day was Saturday, a half holiday—and we ate it sitting on a mossy fallen tree.

'I don't see how it could be possible to be happier,' said Hugo.

I felt the same. If only Alice were here with us too!

'Yet I wish that we were brothers,' he went on, making queer contact with a half-formed thought in my own mind. 'Toby: I was reading the other night about a ceremony performed by some tribes in the Balkan lands. To make a closer alliance between two friends, they become sworn brothers. Then from that day their whole families are related—brothers, cousins, parents—as if they were indeed connected by blood.'

'What is the ceremony?' I asked. My heart was beating strangely, so that my tongue felt thick and my voice was husky.

'Oh, it is very simple—both men tie a string round their finger until it swells up. Then the finger is pricked, and a drop of blood allowed to fall on to a piece of bread, or a lump of sugar. Then each man eats the other's bread or sugar. And they swear brotherhood for evermore.'

I said, trembling, 'Shall we do that, Hugo? You and I?'

'Have you any string?' he said.

'Of course!'

I always carried string, for tying up bundles of plants or (as was occasionally necessary) for mending Fanny's aged harness. I pulled out a tangle of it from my pocket and we each tied a piece round a fore-finger. Hugo's fingers were long and skinny; it took a long time for the blood to congest. But at last it did so. He pulled a pin from his neckerchief and plunged it in. I did the same. We had ready two lumps of sugar from Fanny's bribe-supply and allowed the drops of blood to fall on them, watching as the red liquid dissolved in the gritty brown stuff. Then we exchanged lumps and solemnly ate them.

'I swear to be your brother, Toby, from this day on.'

'And I swear to be yours, Hugo, for ever.'

I stared into his pale face, topped with that incandescent thatch of yellow, and suddenly the gravity of the ritual overcame me, and I burst into a shout of laughter. Hugo did the same, and we rolled off the log into the bluebells, wrestling and cuffing one another . . .

On the way home, Hugo said, 'Now Alice is *my* sister, just as much as yours.'

For a moment, this announcement made me queerly angry; I did not reply. But soon, looking sideways, I saw that Hugo was made anxious by my silence, so I answered in an easy tone, 'That is true, Hugo,' as if I had given the matter careful thought.—Which, God knows, I had.

I suppose it might have been the following year when Hugo said, 'Why should we not go and visit your sister Alice?'

By now the mule, Fanny, had died of old age, and had been replaced by a stout and short-legged cob, of a more willing and active nature; otherwise such a scheme would not have been practicable. But, as matters were, we thought that, if we got up early on a Saturday (Fortune favouring us, Mr Ellis had gone for a fortnight to visit his mother in Exeter, and left us with various assignments to finish on our own) the journey to and from Tunbridge Wells need not take more than a couple of hours each way. Or possibly three.

We set off early without telling anybody our intention. By now I was thirteen, Hugo fifteen; we were quite old enough, in our own opinion, to travel such a distance by ourselves; but in my heart I felt very certain that if we had mentioned our plan to any adult in the family there would have been an outcry of disapproval and prohibition. So, as was our custom, we proceeded quietly on our way, having first obtained a packet of food from Agnys.

Hugo was in high spirits. And, indeed, so was I. The sight of new, unknown country was exhilarating. And then there was the happy prospect ahead—

'At last I am to see Alice!' he said. 'I do so wonder what she will look like. Does Sophy resemble her at all, Toby, do you think?'

Sophy, now ten, was growing a very pretty girl, with a pert little nose, a ready smile, and a cluster of dark curls all over her head.

I said, 'No. No. I do not think so. Alice—Alice had a *special* look. Not pretty, precisely; but when you looked into her face you saw her whole heart.'

My voice faltered. I wondered if this might be a terribly foolish thing that we were doing; if the Wakehursts would be furious with us, if Alice herself would consider it improper behaviour ... as we passed milepost after milepost my heart sank lower and lower. And the journey lasted much longer than we had anticipated; by the time we had reached the outskirts of Tunbridge Wells, the hour was well past noon.

The town lies in a kind of basin, surrounded by high, heathy country. Jerrom Bayes had described to me, often enough, where the Wakehursts' house was situated, and we had no difficulty in locating it, asking our way, and aided by his account of 'a large modern mansion with a wrought-iron fence'.

Arrived at the place, I said, 'Perhaps I had best inquire at the door, Hugo, while you wait here with the trap.'

I could see that he was not wholly content with this scheme but, reluctantly, he said, 'Very well. Do not be long!' and positioned the gig where he could see me as I approached the front door.

After I had rung the bell there followed a long pause, then at last a sluttish, sleepy-looking maidservant opened the door.

'What is it?' said she, rubbing her eyes and yawning.

'I—Is Miss Alice Lamb at home?'

'Miss Alice *Who*—oh!—you mean Miss Alice? I never

heard her called *Lamb*. No, she bain't at home.' And the girl was closing the door in my face when, utterly disappointed and cast down, but still hoping that this would prove to be a mere temporary setback, I asked, 'When will she return?'

'Lord bless you, not for a pig's month! They've all gone to Paris!'

Now with my tail truly between my legs I returned dejectedly to Hugo and informed him that we had come on a fool's errand.

'Well, as we are here, let us at least look at Tunbridge Wells,' he proposed; but when we considered the late hour, we realised that, even if we turned round at once and made for home at our cob's best possible pace, we must still be extremely late for dinner, and the story of our excursion was bound to emerge.

'I wonder why Jerrom didn't tell me?' I pondered, as our poor cob plodded the long miles, less interesting to us now because we had travelled them before. 'He must have known. The girl said they'd been gone two months.'

'He didn't tell you because then he'd lose his penny-a-week,' pointed out Hugo. 'He gives the letters to the maid, I suppose.'

I supposed so too. It is always disheartening when a person that one had thought to be a friend turns out to have been prompted by motives of self-interest.

'I am so disappointed not to have seen Alice,' said Hugo.

Disappointed? That word was utterly inadequate to describe the hot grief, the desolation, the ineffectual rebellious misery that surged within my breast. For the last week I had thought of little else. I had dwelt in my mind so much on seeing Alice, on discovering if she was well, was happy; I felt, as it were, personally rejected, I felt as if enemies had deliberately set this trap for me and were now laughing at my discomfiture.

And, of course, when we arrived home, late, hungry, and dusty, we were in terrible trouble. My father was particularly angry, and even Grandmother Grebell had no word to say in our defence.

'How came you to embark on such a hare-brained course? Everybody here at home has been worried to death about you, wondering where you had got to, if you were dead in some channel of the marsh; to go off like that without even inquiring as to whether such a visit would be welcome or acceptable—it is the outside of enough! Ill-bred—imprudent—ill-conditioned—no one would think you had been gently brought up—'

I was soundly beaten by my father who said that, if it rested with him, he would deprive us of our pony-carriage, since we were not responsible enough to make sensible use of it. Such a trip was far too much for the cob—look at him! dead lame—and suppose the Wakehursts had been at home, what in the world would they have done with us?

'It was a most ill-judged escapade, and greatly impairs the better opinion I was beginning to form of you,' he pronounced, and Robert sniggered every time he encountered me, and sang 'How many miles to Tunbridge Wells?' in a very annoying manner.

Hugo escaped without punishment, for Uncle Allen was never one to scold, though he did say mildly that it had been a very foolish scheme, and that confinement to the bounds of Rye while the cob recovered from his lameness would, he hoped, be sufficient reminder to us that we must learn to think more carefully before again embarking on such a venture.

When I went to say goodnight to my mother that evening, she whispered (for by now she could not speak aloud) 'Toby, it was wrong of you to try to visit Alice. And you are justly served that she was not there.'

'I am sorry, ma'am. It was just—it was just that I longed so to see her.'

Tired and miserable, I laid my head down for a moment on the bed-cover. She moved her hand a little so that the fingers just touched my cheek.

'Poor Toby. I know what you feel. Only a heart of stone would not. But it is better that Alice was not there. Think how she must have felt if she had been: that you were free to come and go, whereas she—'

My mother coughed a little, painfully, and continued after a moment,

'Also, she would see that luck has favoured you these last few years. You have grown stronger—healthier. But suppose—suppose Alice has not been so lucky? Because of your improvement? Such things may be . . .' And she added, as if to herself, 'I pray God that this affliction of mine is what keeps James sound and well—'

'Ma'am, what can you mean? Surely one person's good health could not mean another's misfortune?'

Yet I could remember my grandmother saying something of a similar kind about the balance between members of one family.

My father came angrily into the bedchamber as if he had heard his name spoken.

'Minnie!' (so he sometimes addressed my mother) 'you are not to be tiring yourself in this way. Toby, go to bed. And it will be dry bread for your breakfast.'

'Yes, Father.'

I crept to bed with a heavy heart, aware that my father had flung himself down, in the place that I had just left, and was crying, 'Minnie, Minnie, how can I bear it? What shall I ever do without you?'

Robert, as the eldest, now had a room to himself, and I now shared with Moses and seven-year-old Jem. But they were both asleep, for which I was thankful.

Hugo's and my next escapade, if it can be called that, was far more serious. It still makes me groan with anguish to recall it. And yet, thank God, the plan was, in the first place, initiated by my father. So that, in the outcome, being just, though severe, he could not blame us nearly so much as he blamed himself.

Moses had his birthday in December, not long before Christmas. He would be nine. Like Robert, he was a lively, active lad, more interested in riding, fishing, bowling hoops, coursing hares, or football, than in his lessons. Yet he was far more intelligent than Robert, worked well at his books when he must, and had taken to following Hugo and me about (when he could catch us) and asking endless questions on all manner of topics.

Hugo's behaviour with the younger children was curious. He could, if he so wished, entertain them most delightfully—hold them spellbound, indeed—with all manner of contrivances, games, verbal tricks, and fancies; in ten minutes he would think of more things to say and do with them than would cross my mind in as many days or weeks. And yet, he was not really fond of them. 'There, that is enough,' he would cry out impatiently, after performing prodigies of wit and invention, 'Run away, now, get along with you, don't bother me any more.' He would not care if he saw no more of them for weeks, or, indeed, ever again. And yet the children never seemed to discover this lack of fondness in him; they would cluster around and pester him for songs and riddles as soon as he appeared.

I have heard it said that children have a natural instinct for knowing who loves them and who does not; judging from the behaviour of our young ones to Hugo I am able to give that theory the lie. Yet he was never unkind to them; simply, he made it plain that he did not wish for their company.

Moses had often begged to accompany Hugo and me

on one of our expeditions and we had always refused him on the perfectly valid grounds that our father would never allow it.

'He would say you are too little for such outings. Besides, you would be a nuisance, you would grow tired, and become bored, and whine and complain.'

'No, I would not! I am sure I would not!'

On their birthdays the children were always allowed some indulgence, a visit to a Punch-and-Judy, an excursion to Winchelsea Castle, or whatever; so when it became time for Moses to choose his treat, he asked to go out with Hugo and me.

'For I shall be nine. You cannot say that I shall be too small then!'

Moses had worked hard (for him) at school during the previous months, and my father was inclined to grant his request. Hugo and I were in good odour again; our truancy to Tunbridge Wells was forgotten; many months had passed since then.

I argued strongly against taking Moses out with us. Hugo, I knew, did not wish it.

'Sir, it is the winter. It will be too cold for him in the open pony-trap. He will soon be sorry that he ever asked to come; and then he will start to grumble and wish to be taken home. And—another thing—he is so excitable and hard to manage.'

This was true.

'If he gets some freak into his head he can be as wild and unruly as a young colt,' I said. And this also was true. Moses had the sweetest temper in the world, was kind as could be to his sister Sophy and little Jem, but, let him grow at all excited, and he seemed to lose all control or sense, whirled about, laughed and shouted, lifted heavy weights that might have seemed impossible for a boy of his size, and broke things that he afterwards bitterly regretted.

'Well,' said my father drily, 'it will be up to you and Hugo to see that he does *not* become over-excited. You and Hugo in general have things as you like them to a degree which, for boys of your age, I consider ill-advised—and have often said as much to your Uncle Allen; now let us see how you can handle a bit of responsibility. For, after all, it will not be long now until you have to assume such cares.'

Yes, I thought rather mutinously, but the responsibility for a family of children is one care that I shall never have to handle, and that, Father, is thanks to you.

However my father's will was law, and Moses had his way. I read him a great lecture, beforehand, upon not behaving himself too boisterous or turbulent, and he made me a most solemn promise that he would not. Indeed, when he took his seat in the trap, he had such a sober and mournful demeanour that Hugo burst out into a fit of laughter and said he looked as if he were on his way to his own execution.

'They used to hang criminals in chains along this road, did you know that?' Hugo added, as we took the highway to Winchelsea. 'A man called Thomas Robinson was hanged up just hereabouts for poisoning his wife with some broken glass.'

And he went on to tell of other such crimes and punishments which he had recently been reading about in an old history of the town. Moses, meanwhile, listened most respectfully and seriously, preserving the same melancholy and attentive countenance. Seeing which Hugo, all of a sudden, burst into song—'Hangman, hangman, slack your rope!' and 'They call me Hanging Johnny!' and other ditties of a like nature, picked up from the sailors on the wharfside, until Moses was laughing and joining in, and the penitential atmosphere quite done away with.

The previous night had been bitterly cold, so that braziers had to be kept burning in the brewery all night, for fear the tubs of wort should grow chill and the yeast plant die. And the day was no warmer: frost, thick as snow, lay white all over the marsh, seamed and criss-crossed with the pale-brown banks of sedge and rush marking the lines of dykes. No hedgerow birds sang, but we could hear the far-away cry of gulls and curlews, and a great heron, flapping by, sang out his call of 'Frank! Frank! Frank!' The sky was bitter grey but a small red sun was sometimes to be seen, fleetingly and low down.

Two days previously there had been a gale, and our plan was to go to the strand, searching for what might there be found in the way of wrack and flotsam, driftwood, spars, and other such treasures. Indeed this was in no way a serious educational outing but one, we thought, better adapted to the capacities of Moses.

Agnys had provided us with a large mince-pie apiece and, on the advice of Gabriel, had poured a dribble of brandy into each pie. ' 'Twill warm the lads,' Gabriel said. 'Though properly, mind, 'twould be best to pour half a glassful of brandy into their boots. Brandy in boots is wonderful warming for the feet.' But Agnys said she was not going to waste brandy in any such sinful manner.

Reaching the upper tidemark we dismounted, leaving the pies in the cart for the moment, and Bendigo the cob tethered to a great baulk of timber that had been flung up on the shingle.

'Now,' said Hugo, who tended to be very authoritative on such occasions, 'I will search along by the edge of the sea; you, Toby, take the high-water-mark, and, Moses, you go in the middle.'

So we started off. The tide was full out, and a huge expanse of icy, shining sand lay exposed, scattered over, here and there, with debris from the storm. It was so cold that the sea's rim was frozen, which I had never seen before, and huge slabs of ice made a white frieze down by the water's edge.

As there was such a wide expanse of empty beach we were, of necessity, far apart, and I could see that Moses began to feel rather lonesome and forlorn, isolated as he was midway between us with several hundred yards gap on either side. This was not what he had bargained for at all, poor lad. At first he walked along briskly enough, looking about him; but, after a mile or so, he began to lag, and to droop his head, and drag his feet.

I had said to Hugo beforehand, 'Moses will soon become bored, I daresay,' and he had replied briskly, 'So much the better. Then he will not always be begging to come with us on future occasions.' I wondered if this arrangement of Hugo's, stationing us so far apart, had been done with deliberation, and concluded that almost certainly it had; most of Hugo's actions were very deliberate.

Though of course the final outcome was in no way what he had intended.

I began to pity poor Moses, wandering along so dejectedly with his hands in his pockets (he had evidently not found anything that he considered worth picking up) so I called to him, 'Do you want to come up here and help me search?' and he ran to me with alacrity. There were, in fact, better pickings up here on the high tideline, and he soon had the satisfaction of pouncing on a lady's ivory fan, slightly broken, while I found a small wooden tub of cheese, a feather-bed (too sodden with salt water to be worth salvaging), the shaft of an anchor, and a pair of fire-tongs.

Moses presently began to complain that he ached with cold; his teeth were chattering and he looked blue and pinched. I did not wish him to become ill from his birthday outing, so I said to him, 'Why don't you run back to the cart with these things'—giving him the cheese and the tongs—'run fast, that will warm you. Meanwhile Hugo and I will go on another quarter-mile'—I knew Hugo would not wish to turn back so soon—'then we will search in the other direction. Run really fast, now!'

Moses nodded, shivering—he was a champion runner among his cronies—took the objects, and scudded off along the pale, shining beach. I waved to Hugo, gesturing at Moses, and saw him shrug, as to say, what did I expect? So, after another quarter-mile, I signalled to Hugo again, indicating that I now intended to turn round. I walked down to the middle of the beach and followed along the line that Moses had searched, in a reverse direction, finding a cracked wooden bowl that he had overlooked, and a glass bottle that he had probably rejected, as it was broken.

By the time that I reached the pony-trap Moses was dancing about gaily enough; he had wrapped round his shoulders an old red cloak of my grandmother's that we had brought along to keep our legs warm on the journey.

He seemed in much better spirits, and when I went to put my troves in the cart, I discovered the reason why.

'Moses! You've never eaten *all three* of those mince-pies?'

He hung his head and muttered, 'I—I am sorry, brother Toby. I ate one—and then—and then—they were so good—I couldn't stop!' He added defensively, 'It *is* my birthday!'

'You little wretch! What about us? I'll give you such a trouncing—!' I exclaimed, only half in earnest, and started towards him. He then let out a screech of pretended terror, and ran away from me, giggling, up the shingle-slope towards the distant sand-hills.

I turned to ascertain where Hugo had got to before giving chase, and saw that he was halfway along the beach,

73

watching us. I made gestures to indicate that I was going in pursuit of Moses, and did so.

The latter, by this time, was thoroughly enjoying the chase. I heard him panting and laughing and calling, 'You'll not catch me! You'll never catch me!' and he bounded about like a dervish, waving his arms and the red cloak, scampering up and down the cold slippery sides of the sand-hills. At least, I thought, he was getting warm and was enjoying himself.

Whether Hugo realised that Moses had committed some misdemeanour, or thought that it was just a game that we were playing, he evidently intended to take part, and so he ran through the sand-hills farther along the shore, with the evident intention of taking Moses in the rear. Hugo, with his skinny height, could run much faster than I. My lameness was still a slight disability when running, though I could walk well enough.

Hugo was soon out of sight; I, meanwhile, went on with my pursuit of Moses, which was not difficult (although I could not at present see him) because of his tracks in the sand.

Beyond the sand-hills lay a wide belt of pebbly shingle, and beyond that extended the marsh, partly grass, partly mudbanks, with pools of water, and lawns of sea-lavender and kale, and patches of thrift, and sea-asparagus, samphire, glasswort, all the other succulent plants that thrive in places where salt water comes and goes. But today, because of the extreme cold, this area was covered all over with white frost and shone ghostly and dimly in the grey light. Further inland, as I knew, ran a couple of channels, quite deep, which emptied into the sea a mile to westwards; in order to reach the strand we had been obliged to make a detour to the east and cross a couple of wooden bridges.

So the retreat of Moses would be cut off; unless he dodged Hugo and fled far along to the bridges.

'Moses!' I called. 'Stop! It doesn't matter! Leave off running. I am not so angry as all that—it is your birthday after all. Come back!'

I could see him again, not too far away, crossing the shingle with some difficulty, slipping and stumbling. Men who get their living by gleaning from the beaches walk with boards called backstays tied to their feet, on these shingle-beds, which stretch for miles in some parts. Moses, having no boards, was in difficulty, but at last he gave a great leap, and gained the farther side. Then he turned, beaming, to wave his red cloak at me in triumph.

Not until that moment had he noticed Hugo who, having circled round the side of a sand-dune, was now much closer to him than I was.

At that instant the sun, revealed by a gap in the grey overcast sky, suddenly shone forth a great golden beam which dazzlingly illuminated the white-and-grey landscape, the frosty sand-hills, the frozen marsh. Hugo, full in the light of this beam, tall and slender with his shock of pale-yellow hair, looked, I suppose, like some avenging angel, especially as just then he raised his hands in an attitude of pretended menace. I heard Moses give a shriek of laughing terror—even then it was mostly pretence—and he began to run once more, making a wide arc so as to avoid Hugo's line of attack.

But what neither of them noticed, because they had eyes only for each other, but which I beheld with horror, was one of those intractable bulls, which some farmers keep at pasture on the marsh, because few folk go there, and they are not so likely to be troubled with complaint about the danger and ferocity of the animals. They range freely about the marsh and, in general, it is not too difficult to avoid them, by keeping a sharp lookout beforehand.—This specimen, a huge black brute with a massive breadth of chest above nimble little legs, and two sickle-shaped white horns, had evidently been aroused by all our shouts, and was making its way, at a deceptively smooth fast trot, towards Moses.

'MOSES!' I yelled. 'Come this way. *Quick!* Look out for the *bull!*'

He turned, saw the menace behind him, gasped in terror, and started to run quickly in my direction.

The bull, behind him, broke into a gallop. I could see that it would easily overtake him before he reached me.

He also realised this, and turned again, desperately, in the other direction, while Hugo and I both ran from different points towards the bull, waving our arms, shouting, hoping to divert its attention.

It paused, looked at us, but again turned in pursuit of Moses, attracted, perhaps, by the flapping of the red cloak which he still wore capelike round his shoulders.

Then I noticed another peril ahead of him—a smooth expanse of white.

'*Moses!* For God's sake take care of the channel—'

But without taking heed of my cry, Moses ran frantically away over that flat whiteness, which was not sand but ice—a thin crust over one of the channels running parallel to the beach.

The ice cracked—I had known it could not be very thick, the current running below was too swift—and Moses vanished from view into a black hole of water.

The bull, bellowing with frustration, reached the bank of the channel and stood there, pawing the ground, staring about, shaking its massive head.

I looked round me for a rope, a bar, a spar, an oar—but there was nothing.

Hugo, with crazy courage, began to decoy the bull further away from the spot, shouting, whistling, and waving his arms, until, more slowly now, puzzled by the disappearance of its first quarry, it turned and went after him.

Meanwhile I raced to the spot where Moses had gone under.

Neither Hugo nor I could swim. Sea-bathing, more popular now, was not then in vogue. And Dr Wright had strictly forbidden us to swim in the Rother, or the Tillingham river, as some boys did, for he held that the waters of these streams were aguish and would bring on a recurrence of all our former troubles.

Nevertheless I walked into the water until it reached my chin, feeling wildly about with my arms in the water, which was unbelievably cold, and ran with great swiftness. Calling, sobbing, and gulping, I groped and probed, breaking more of the ice, working down-channel from where Moses had gone in.

'Moses, where are you? Moses, speak to me! *Moses!*'

At last, by pure chance, for my hands had long since lost the power to feel anything, I caught, in my gropings, a corner of the red cloak. Venturing out into midstream with my head under water I was able, grabbing and flailing, to encounter and catch hold of a limb—I could not tell if it were arm or leg. Dragging with all my strength, digging my heels in the slippery bottom, holding my breath, I pulled on what felt an impossible weight.

'Hold on, I'm coming!' I heard Hugo shout, as my head emerged above water, and then he was there in the stream, helping me, we each had an arm of Moses and were hauling him to the side of the channel. Hoisting him up the bank was a seemingly impossible task; yet somehow, in the end, we did it.

'Moses, speak! Can you speak?'

But he did not speak. His head lolled, with water coming out of the open mouth. His eyes were shut.

'We must turn him over and beat on his back,' gasped

Hugo, and so we did that. More water ran from his mouth, but he neither spoke nor moved. We stared at one another, speechless with horror.

'I—I will bring the cart,' said Hugo, after a moment, in a broken voice. 'If we can get him home quickly enough—perhaps Dr Wright—if he is put to bed at once—'

We both knew, I think, from the start, that nothing would make any difference, that the matter was hopeless, and yet we both, on the way home, kept up a kind of wretched pretence, hurrying poor Bendigo (who was eager enough, heaven knew, to get back to his warm stable). We had covered Moses with most of our sodden clothes, and the cloak, and laid him on the floor of the cart.

When we reached the foot of Mermaid Street, Hugo said hoarsely, 'I will go ahead and—and tell Agnys, tell her to get Grandma Grebell—' His voice broke at the thought, but he squared his shoulders resolutely and set off walking at a fast pace up the hill.

Even now I cannot bear to think of the aftermath of that day. As I have said, my father was just, if stern; he did not unreasonably blame us. If Agnys had not poured brandy into the pies, if Moses had not eaten them all three—if the bull had not appeared just at that moment, if the ice had not broken—The *ifs* were endless, but none of them, in the end, made any difference.

At one point my father said to Hugo, 'How did you manage to get rid of the bull? So as to go back and help Toby?'

'Oh, I went very close to him and managed to entice him out on to the ice—at a point, upstream, where it was thicker. It broke under him and so I managed to escape while he was floundering in the water. He did not drown, I suppose bulls can swim, but the soaking seemed to quench his wish to come after us any more.'

I noticed my father give Hugo a long queer look. 'I

see,' he said. 'I wondered how you had given him the
slip.' He said no more. He had never greatly liked Hugo,
but after that he treated him with a kind of cold respect.

As for me ... I could see that for months after
the tragedy my father could hardly bear to look at me.

If only, he was visibly thinking, if only it had been
Toby who drowned, and not Moses, who was bright,
quick, active, goodnatured, and had nothing to prevent
him becoming the progenitor of a long line of Lambs.

Both Hugo and I caught colds, narrowly avoided
inflammation of the lungs, and were confined to bed
for several weeks after the disaster, so were unable to see
one another. I was moved downstairs to one of the guest
chambers, where it was easier for Dr Wright to visit me,
and lay in solitary misery, for the most part.

Sometimes Grandma Grebell sat with me, but never
for very long.

'Toby,' she said once, 'it is hard on you. You will just
have to bear it as best you can. Now: for your ears alone:
I think that Moses would, sooner or later, have come to
grief. He was too vehement, always.'

'Sooner or later—' I mumbled. 'But why did it have
to be *sooner*? Why did it have to be with me?'

Sophy never visited my bedside. Moses had been her
special brother. When smaller, they had been inseparable,
and even latterly they had spent all the time together that
they could manage, considering that Sophy had now been
taken out of school and was hard at work learning, as Alice
had, the arts of housewifery.

One very startling thing did happen to me while
I was laid up in bed.

I had a letter from my sister Alice.

I had written to her, as soon as I could put pen to
paper, pouring out the wretched tale, and had despatched
the latter, as usual, by the hand of Jerrom Bayes, never

thinking to have a reply. For all I knew the Wakehursts were still in France. But it was my habit, now, to express my feelings to Alice and, despite the fact that she never answered, I could not stop. To write the story down eased my agony a little.

And then one evening, with my supper broth, to my great amazement Agnys handed me a small folded paper.

'Jerrom give me this for you, Toby boy. Reckon 'tis a letter from Miss Alice after all this long time. What's she say, then?'

Poor Agnys felt bitterly remorseful about the brandy in the pies. Her way of atonement was to show me all the sympathy and interest that she could. She remained by the bed while I read the brief note.

'Dear Brother I am very sorry to hear of poor Moses and your trouble. A heart of stone would ache. I feel for you sincerely. Your sister, Alice.'

It was rather carelessly written, with several mistakes.

'Well, she don't waste words, do she,' commented Agnys with a sniff. 'Nor ink nor paper neither.' She paused a moment, then added thoughtfully, 'Ask me, it's right queer she wouldn't write more? Miss Alice used to be that tender-hearted—and she were main fond of you, Master Toby. You'd think she'd bestir herself to write a longer letter?'

'Maybe they keep her busy all the time, those Wakehursts.'

'Money be the root of all ill,' said Agnys, taking my soup bowl.

I tucked the little note under my pillow. And that night when I endured again the dreadful dream, reliving again for the hundredth time the happenings by the channel, when I woke and lay trembling with utter misery, my only wish not to be Toby Lamb, not to be here, that the past two weeks had never happened, the thought of Alice's letter under my lumpy flock pillow comforted me, just a little.

I never told Hugo that I had received it.

When I saw him next, when we were both pronounced fit enough to resume our lessons—which we did most thankfully—there seemed no fit opportunity to tell him. And as time stretched on, it began to seem impossible. There was no way, no way at all, in which I could have said, 'Oh, by the bye, Hugo, I had a letter from my sister Alice.' So I kept it to myself.

Two more years passed, peaceably enough. Robert, now seventeen, had left school and entered the brewery. Robert would never have requested a college education.—But, as matters fell out, he did not particularly enjoy his work at the brewery either. Work never pleased Robert. What he wanted was money in his pocket, and a group of admiring friends always round him.

After the death of Moses my father began to develop a pair of deep grooves, which ran from his nostrils to the corner of his mouth, and a similar, vertical pair between his brows. Yet James Lamb was hardly forty, a man approaching the prime of life. Little Jem, now eight, was his hope and joy.

Hugo had been entered for Cambridge, and would commence his studies there in the Michaelmas term. I, two years younger, must wait at least another year, and the prospect of my life without Hugo's company every day was bleak indeed. Uncle Allen still referred to us as 'Orestes and Pylades'—though our friendship had, perhaps, grown a little less open and sunny than in former years, because of the death of Moses. That occurrence had caused silences between us.

I missed Moses more than I could say. He had been a lively, laughing presence about Lamb House, always ready with a word, a question, a joke, a song, an offer of help. Moses had never been spiteful in his life, or unkind, or deliberately naughty. He had often mediated between my father (who, though just, was a stern disciplinarian, and somewhat lacking in humour) and other members of the family.

My sorrow for Moses went deep, and yet I could see that Hugo did not share it. He had never sought to know the boy, or taken any notice of him.—This was due to no lack of kindliness on Hugo's part: simply, he could not take interest in someone so much younger than himself. Our friendship, Hugo's and mine, I sometimes felt, was based on a lucky accident, that I was the first person he met, on arriving in this land.

The end of my childhood occurred, not over a period of time, but in a sudden cataclysm. The events, interconnected, which led to this, I will now relate.

I can remember with clarity how it all began, on a Saturday in September. As on a previous occasion I was at work in the little cobbled yard to the west of Lamb House, splitting billets of wood, this time, in preparation for the coming winter. Splitting wood is a peaceful task, if carried on at one's own pace in a leisurely manner. It is done with a mallet-hammer and a tolerably heavy iron wedge. No great strength is required, the art is more in selecting the correct spot, where the wood is weakest. At the sawn-off end of the billet there will always be some tiny crack or fissure, just discernible; into this your wedge must be gently tapped and firmed; then one clinching blow often suffices to crack the whole log from end to end, while the iron wedge tumbles out with a clang on to the cobbles.

In this soothing occupation I had been absorbed for some time by myself. Little Jem had wandered out and asked if he might help, and I kindly allowed him to try, well aware that, fortunately, he would not even be able to raise the hammer from the ground; soon he wandered off again to find Sophy and ask if she would take him to the Gun Gardens. Robert, liberated on Saturday afternoon from the brewery, had gone to hare-coursing with a party of friends, observing, as he passed me, that it was 'a pleasure to see me doing something useful once in a way, instead of frittering away my time with books'. To which I made no reply. Hugo, over at Uncle Allen's, was about to set off for an interview of some importance; I would see him later.

As my hands picked up the logs and turned them, and my eyes chose the spot for insertion of the wedge, my thoughts were occupied with a tale which I had it in mind to write.

Hugo and I had been reading Jonathan Swift's master-piece, *Gulliver's Travels*, which Mr Ellis had lent us, and I, filled with emulation, wondered if it would not be possible to write a fiction of a similar satirical kind, yet set among everyday humble folk, not in fantastical lands such as Lilliput and Brobdignag.

So I was content enough, pondering on the outline of my story while searching for the line of weakness in my billets and then, with scientific skill, knocking them in half. (Sometimes the wood resists for a moment or two; you can hear the log let out a little groaning protest as the fibres pull away from one another; and then you wait, patiently, attending, as it were, on the wood's convenience until by instinct you recognise the moment for the final knock that will cleave it from top to bottom.)

I had my hammer uplifted for this clinching stroke when a soft voice from behind me said, 'Toby?'

Turning, I saw a lady standing in the gateway that led to the garden-lane.

To first sight she was very grand, in a frilled, hooped robe with drapings and ruchings and panniers (I know not what)—far finer than anything worn by the ladies in Rye, with a tilted hat over her hair, which was dressed high and powdered, and a braided mantle over her shoulders. Her face, which bore a bright red spot upon either cheekbone, appeared faintly familiar, and I was gazing at her in puzzlement, wondering why she had come to the back gate rather than to the front door, and if she wished to see my father, who was undoubtedly round at the brewery (for Saturdays were never by him taken as in any way different from ordinary working days) when the lady spoke again.

'Don't you know me, Toby?' she said. 'I am Alice.'

'*Alice!*'

I tried to make my voice sound overjoyed, but consternation, I fear, was the dominant note.

Always, through the whole of my childhood, I had, I suppose, against reason, even against instinct, nourished a blind hope that one day Alice would return to me, my own dearly-loved Alice. Some day, some day, it must happen.

Now, not only was I deprived of my Alice, but that hope must be utterly quenched, once for all. This flashily-dressed, careworn, harsh-faced stranger was not my Alice; my Alice had been taken away for ever.

'For—for a moment,' I stammered, 'I did not know you! Even yet, I find it hard to believe. You—you are dressed so fine!'

'Oh—clothes,' she said impatiently.

Of course it was not the clothes. Clothes could not have disguised her. I was now aged fifteen, so Alice, five years older, must, I knew, be twenty. But this lady looked ten, twenty years older even than that. Alice had been endearingly plump. This lady was thin as starvation. Her nose, jaw, and cheekbones, prominent as they had never been before, created a sudden startling resemblance to Grandma Grebell. Her dark ringlets had been exchanged for a cone of thickly powdered grey; impossible to tell what the real colour might be. Alice's countenance had always worn a look of humble friendliness, ready to melt into a smile at the least encouragement; whereas this stranger's look was hard, wary, and utterly disillusioned.

Yet she did smile, a brief quirk of the mouth, as she eyed me.

'You have grown so straight, Toby. And not bad looking. Fancy! I would not have believed it possible. Where is my own little lame lad?'

Her voice, too, was shriller than I had remembered. Very likely, I thought, she is, in her way, as disappointed as I in mine. I stood up, and clasped her hands; I would have kissed her, but she drew her head away.

'No: you will spoil my paint.'

Paint! 'Is Cousin Honoria with you?' I asked, rebuffed, 'and Captain Wakehurst? Shall I call my father?'

'No, I am alone,' she said. 'Wait: don't call Father yet. I have come home for good, Toby. Will you help me fetch my baggage? Or tell Gabriel to fetch it? My things were too heavy to carry; I left them at the coach stop.'

'Good heaven!' I stared at her, wholly overthrown by this news. 'You have *come home to live here*?'

'Well? You don't sound very happy about it? Here you have been writing me all these letters, all these years—"Alice I miss you," "Alice I wish you could come back"—and now that I have come back you seem displeased. Aren't you glad to see me?'

'No—no, Alice, no I am—of course I am happy—' I stammered. 'It is just so—it is the unexpectedness.—Then you *did* receive my letters—all of them? From the very beginning?'

'Oh yes. Oh yes, I received them.' Her voice sounded angry again. 'They were all read aloud to me. Most faithfully.'

'But—but I don't understand—*do* explain, Alice dear.' With a huge effort, I tried to re-create the former bond there had been between us, tried to make it as it had been before. 'Why are you come home, so suddenly? With no warning? Did you have a falling-out with Cousin Honoria? With Captain Wakehurst?'

'He is dead,' she said baldly. 'And Cousin Honoria has been ill. But is better now.'

'Dead? Captain Wakehurst?' I was thunderstruck. 'Of what cause?'

'Thrown by his horse out hunting.' She said with a curious dispassion, 'He always was a bruising rider.'

'Hunting—so early in the season?'

'No, this was last March. Now Cousin Honoria is to marry again, and she does not want me any longer. Or at least her future husband does not. We should not suit, as house-mates. So I have my orders to trudge. I should constitute a disagreeable reminder,' said Alice with curling lip, 'of bygone times.'

A number of questions jostled together in my head, yet I hardly dared ask any of them. (I was reminded—somehow, most strangely—of groping in the icy channel for the dead, outflung hand of Moses. I had the same sensation of desperate, hopeless search in an awful wilderness; of expecting the very worst.)

'Did—did they use you kindly, Alice?' I at last asked, in a timid voice.

'No,' she said. 'No. They used me very ill.'

Her dark brown eyes stared into mine, but they were opaque; I could not read their message.

'But it is over now,' she added after a pause. 'And Cousin Honoria, as I said, is to marry again—she is to marry a gentleman who is, in every way, as different as he can be from Captain Wakehurst: the Reverend Samuel Gates. A very devout, saintly, and Christian gentleman.

He hopes to become the father of a thriving family. And, of course, he has many Christian and charitable plans for the disposition of Cousin Honoria's fortune.'

'But,' I said stupidly, thinking that if Captain Wakehurst had come to his end last March—and why in the world had nobody taken the trouble to inform us of this event?—if he had died in March, here it was September, Cousin Honoria had been almost scandalously speedy in selecting another partner. 'But I thought Cousin Honoria was—was unable to bear children? Was not that why she adopted you?'

'That proved to be a mistake,' said Alice in a very dry tone. 'The fault, it seemed, lay in the gentleman, not in the lady.'

I wondered how they could know such a thing. 'But in any case, surely, now, she is by far too old to bear children?'

'Well,' said Alice, 'that we shall soon see. And if she dies in childbirth—why, then Mr Gates will be a rich widower.'

She stared restlessly round her at the little yard. It was a humble, friendly enclosure; the cobbles were littered with chips and splinters from my activities; wallflowers and valerian grew against the brick wall of the house; the late sun threw down sloping rays, which were spangled with tiny midges.

'So many, many times,' said Alice, 'I thought I should never see this place again. Well: I am glad I have. It does not seem to have changed. It even feels welcoming.—How is my mother? Shall I go in and see her?'

She moved towards the door.

I said in haste, 'Dear Alice, I am afraid she is very ill. Her appearance will be a shock to you.'

But hardly so much, I thought, as yours to her. Still, I could not forbid Alice to visit the sickroom; though I thought it more than possible my father might do so.

Yet Alice lingered.

'Where is Grandmother Grebell?'

'She had a fall three weeks ago. Her hip broke. She is obliged to keep her bed, in Uncle Allen's house.'

'What a pity.' Alice's tone was somewhat perfunctory. I thought her regret lay chiefly in the fact that our grandmother would not be there to act as a bulwark between herself and our parents. In confirmation of which, she said,

'The thought of seeing Mother frightens me. Oh well—I had best get it over—'

She spoke with a sort of resolute hardihood, utterly different from the old timid Alice, and walked quickly in at the back door, calling over her shoulder, 'You will see after my bags, will you not, Toby?'

I went and fetched the bags, making three journeys of it, for there were a great number, and carried them into the kitchen. There I found Agnys and Polly (both big-eyed and wan, as if they had come from a funeral) engaged in an agitated, low-voiced conversation.

'Is Alice upstairs?' I asked, interrupting. 'Is she with my mother? Do you think I should put her bags in one of the guest chambers? She can hardly sleep in the attic now, with Sophy?'

'Oh, Master Toby!' gasped Agnys. 'Oh, Master Toby!' And then she flung her apron over her head and fairly burst out crying. There were tracks of tears, too, on Polly's weatherbeaten cheeks.

'That I should live to see this day,' Agnys sobbed. 'When I think of the little thing she was—so taking in her ways—my poor little missie.'

Wordless, I hugged Agnys. What comfort could I offer? There was nothing to be said. After a moment I detached myself and carried a couple of the bags upstairs, for I thought it not advisable that Alice should remain with my mother for too long. Indeed, as I reached the top stair I heard a low wail from my mother's chamber, and saw Alice appear looking white and shocked—though the bright red patch still burned, like a poppy, on either cheekbone.

'Oh, she is *so ill*—I did not know. *Why* did you not tell me?' she muttered.

I had told her many times, but I suppose nobody believes a story until they see the proof of it for themselves.

'Look, Alice, I will put your things in here. And now I will go over to the brewery and find Father.'

Polly and Agnys ran upstairs with bundles of clean linen, and Agnys went at once into Mother's room; I heard her scolding and exclaiming.

With a heavy heart I went to the brewery and told Father the news.

At first he could hardly take it in.

'Sent her *back*? Like a parcel of unwanted goods? How dare they?'

'Well, Captain Wakehurst is dead, it seems—he broke his neck out hunting—and Cousin Honoria is to marry again, so Alice says—'

'She lost little time,' snapped Father, echoing my thought. 'And so Alice is to be flung back at us with naught gained but, I daresay, a set of expensive habits. Well for us! Why in the world—during all those years—did they not find her a husband? Has she lost her looks?'

Fuming and muttering, he strode past me. My own spirits, anticipating the imminent confrontation between James Lamb and his daughter, were as low as they could be. Like a coward, I lingered a moment or two in the courtyard of the brewery. Pockets of hops were coming in from the Kentish hopgardens, strapped up tight, with layers of hops packed down inside them as hard as sausage-meat in a sausage, and a wonderful aromatic resinous perfume floating out. Greenish-gold dust blew about from a sample pocket which my father had opened to make sure of the quality. (The hop harvest this year had been somewhat later than usual, but plentiful.) I walked back inside the brick-piered, stone-floored brewery and stood in the dimness among the great bell-shaped vats holding porter, and the hogsheads and kilderkins of lighter beer, wishing, I knew not what: that everything might be different; that I might go back to be a child again. Although I had not been happy as a child.

At last I went over to the house. Dusk was falling as I passed the entrance to the little herb-garden. I thought of the Frenchman. Did he still walk? Was he perhaps there now, and I unable to see him? Were we humans surrounded, all the time, unknowingly, by the spirits of people who had come before us, who had led unhappy lives, had failed, had died, and were still wandering this earth unsatisfied, lamenting their failure, with things that they wished to express, to pass on, to tell us?

Shall I, in my turn, haunt this spot one day?

Entering the house through the kitchen I found Sophy there, with little Jem, she looking as startled as if she, in her turn, had seen the Frenchman's ghost.

'Is that lady *indeed* Sister Alice?' Sophy demanded of me in a whisper. 'She is very fine! But she is not at all as I remember her.'

'Well, you were only four when she went. Yes, it is really Alice. But she has changed into a fine lady.'

'Well I don't like the change,' said Sophy, who could be very downright.

'You will soon become used to it and see the old Alice again,' said I, hoping this might be true.

'She is with my father in his office. He told me to run away,' said Sophy in a complaining tone.

'Doubtless Alice has private things to say to him, and he to her. They won't want me either,' I said, to relieve her grievance, and began to wonder if this would be a moment to step across the road and acquaint Hugo with the news. He had been to spend the day at the house of Mr Ellis, in order to make the acquaintance of his future Cambridge tutor, an ex-fellow-student and old friend of our teacher, who was paying him a visit at present. By now, I thought Hugo must have returned home.

I had not the least eagerness to tell Hugo that Alice was come home. With shame I acknowledged to myself that I did not even wish him to meet this new, hard Alice, so wholly different from all my descriptions; yet the pair must meet, and there was no sense in trying to defer the encounter. They could not be kept apart.

I was walking through the hall to the front door when I heard a cry from upstairs, and Agnys came pattering down the front stairs looking white and terrified.

'Missus has taken such a turn! Toby, be a good boy and run directly for Dr Wright while I tell Master—I'm afeared to leave her more than a moment—'

So I ran to the house of Dr Wright who lived at the corner of East Street and Market Square and who, by great good fortune, was at home and able to return with me. He hurried straight up to my mother's room, where my father now was and, from the hall, I could hear their low, anxious voices.

I went to my father's office, where I found Alice, with head bent and arms folded, staring out of the window at the church, tapping the floor with one scarlet-shod toe.

She looked up as I entered and said, 'What a home-coming!' in a voice that was wretched enough, yet held a hint of irony too. 'Now, I suppose, my father will be able to tell me that I have been the death of our mother.' After a moment or two she added, 'And perhaps it will be true.'

'Is she—is she—?'

'How can I tell?' Alice's face was bleak. 'She certainly looks ready for the next world—'

As if shocked by the sound of her own words, she bit her lip, and pressed the heels of her palms against her cheeks.

I heard the door of Uncle Allen's house slam, and turned to look through the window into the street. Here came Hugo, walking swiftly across the cobbles, his head well up and a lighted, joyful expression on his face.

'Good heavens! Who is *that*?' demanded Alice in a whisper as Hugo reached our front door and, by long custom, came in without knocking.

There was no time for an answer. I called, 'Hugo!' because he was bound to see us through the open office door. 'Step in here and meet my sister Alice who is just come home to us!'

He stood, startled in the doorway, still with that look of radiance and excitement.

'Sister Alice? Really come at last? But what joy! What a wonderful piece of news!'

Turning to Alice I was astounded, almost beyond all measure, to see that Hugo's expression had communicated itself to my sister's face—her cheeks were pink, her eyes bright, she suddenly seemed to blaze with beauty. A moment before, I had been wondering how to apologise for her, how to make excuses for this poor diminished thing who had once been my dear sister—now Hugo gazed at her as if at an angelic vision.

While they talked—he asking if she were come for a day? for a week? and she beginning to explain—I slipped for a moment from the room and ran quietly upstairs.

My father and Dr Wright were in the upper hallway, talking in hushed tones. I hesitated on the top step, not liking to intrude on their discussion with a question, but my father looked round and saw me. His face was dreadful. It reminded me of—what?

'Toby,' he said, 'your mother is no more.'

'Oh, sir!' I drew a deep, ragged breath. How strongly I wished that I had not been running for the doctor at the time of her departure; I wished that I had been at her bedside; yet, what is the use of wishing? And what difference would it have made, had I been there? Yet I wished it. I tried to clasp my father's hands, but he withdrew them quite violently and said, 'You had best—you had best tell the others. Sophy and James. They are below.—Where is Robert?'

'I fear he is out.'

'Where—' my father began, then said, 'No matter. Tell the servants also,' and turned again to the doctor. He was trembling like a galled horse, and I saw the doctor give him a quick look of concern.

With a heart of lead I went first to the office, where Alice and Hugo were talking as if they had known one another for twenty years, instead of five minutes.

I made my announcement and they turned shocked faces to me. Then I excused myself and went off to tell the rest of the household.

Directly after my mother's death my poor father was struck down with a kind of seizure: he became like a child again, weeping and quivering, unable to master himself in any way whatsoever. The doctor administered opiates and Father was, by the combined exertions of Polly, Agnys, and myself, persuaded into bed, where he then remained for upwards of ten days, speechless, tearful, and unable to do anything for himself. He had to be fed with a spoon and washed like a child. Then he suddenly made a complete recovery, arose one morning, dressed himself as usual, came down to breakfast, and never afterwards alluded to his indisposition. It is possible, I think, that he did not even remember it. Nor did he ever speak of my mother, or even inquire about her funeral, which, of course, he had been unable to attend. I am sure that, during her life, he was strongly attached to her. They never talked together but I can remember how sometimes, before she became bedridden, he would sit beside her, silently clasping her hand.—After this brief illness he grew very withdrawn, and spoke only in case of need, never idly. (Though it was a singular fact, and noted by all in the household, that his language had become somewhat coarse; he now used expletives such as By G——! and D——! which would never, before this, have passed his lips.)

The night after my mother died, Alice and I sat up together, in Mother's room, by her motionless draped figure. My father, of course, was abed, slumbering under the doctor's narcotic; Robert had come in very late, and vilely drunk, and, when he heard the news, started to make so lamentable and abominable a disturbance that I could see the only recourse was to give him so large a glass of brandy as to render him insensible. Which I accordingly did. Hugo and my uncle had returned to their own house to impart the sorrowful news to Granny Grebell, and the younger children had cried themselves to sleep. The servants, red-eyed and woebegone (for, even in her extreme illness my mother had been a good mistress) were long retired. But I felt that somebody should attend my mother's last night in the house that had been built for her, to keep her company.

Rather unexpectedly—'I will watch with you,' said Alice, and added, 'In any case, I shall not be able to sleep.—Do you think my father will die also?'

No, I said, the doctor did not think so, and nor did I. By nature, Father was a strong man, he had no sickness in him. This was just a passing weakness.

During that night Alice unfolded to me the history of

what had happened to her at Cousin Honoria's house. The tale is not fit to be told, and I shall not tell it. Alice herself broke off to say from time to time, 'This is no story for your tender ears, Toby; but if I could bear to endure it, I suppose you can bear to listen.'

I could hardly bear to do so, indeed. Many times I had to turn my face away from Alice while she spoke.

I said, 'Why did you not leave them? Run away? Write home for help?'

'Stupid boy! How could I run away? I was only twelve. They would have followed me, taken me back, and used me even worse. Written home? I could not write! They—he—used to read me aloud your letters—'

That thought sent such a piercing shaft of horror through me that I could not speak for some time after. Then I said hoarsely,

'Was there no one to whom you could appeal? Their friends—somebody?'

'Their friends—*his* friends—were as bad. Worse. I could tell you—but I won't! And they told me they had put it around that I was a liar—that I told nothing but lies—they told me it would be useless to try and raise any outcry—for none would believe me—even if I wrote home none would believe me—'

'You did, then, in the end, learn to read and write?'

'Did I not write to you? Oh, yes, *now*,' she said with harsh irony, '*now* I am a different creature from that little, crying, ignorant Alice. They have stolen her from me. They have robbed me of that self for ever.—In the end I learned many things. And the worst lesson of all—that whoever heard my tale would not wish to believe it. You don't believe me—do you, Toby?'

And she gave me a stony look.

'I do believe you,' I protested. 'Of course I do.'

'Not truly. Not at the bottom of your heart. You

wish me to be lying, so that you need not be distressed about me. But this house believes me,' said Alice, looking round at it. By now dawn was beginning to break, a red and threatening sky showed beyond the grey bulk of the church. 'This kindly house welcomes me back,' said Alice. 'It has not changed while you have all changed. You—why, Toby, you have been thriving and doing well, all this long while, with your friend Hugo. You have been happy and cared for—and my father has prospered, I can see—fine new clothes, glossy new furnishings—' She spoke resentfully, as if each change made in her own absence was a kind of betrayal.

'*Don't*, Alice!' I begged. 'It has not all been like that, you don't know! There was the death of Moses—'

'Yes, Moses.' Her voice eased a moment, then hardened again. 'But you had your friend Hugo to comfort you.'

'Don't begrudge me Hugo, pray do not, Alice. I missed you sorely—sorely. I thought I would die of grief.'

'But you did not die, did you, Toby? I have heard them sometimes talking about the slave ships,' said Alice. 'Cousin Honoria's fortune, part of it, derived from the slave trade to the Caribees. I learned how closely those slaves were packed into those vessels. And how many died. And yet there was profit on the rest. And I wondered if the ghosts of those who died will not come back one day to haunt the men who devised such a trade, or their sons. I have been a slave, Toby, do you understand? My rights were no greater than theirs. While you had your freedom—were able to learn—'

'I wrote to you, all those years. Hugo and I tried to come and visit you—but you were not there—'

'Yes, I heard about that. Afterwards.' She laughed, a dry sound. 'Silly children! It is as well that we were in Paris. What a visit *that* would have been!'

'What kind of a city is Paris?' I asked, hoping for some mitigation, some alleviation.

But she said, 'They obliged me to remain in the apartment. I saw nothing of the town. I was their slave, I tell you! Listen, the servants are stirring. Let us go out and walk about Rye.'

So we went down, and out into the little yard. It was a fine cold morning. Frost lay on the moss between the cobbles, and on the splintered wood where I had been at work yesterday. I remembered how peacefully I had busied myself, planning my story. The hammer and wedge still lay where I had dropped them in the woodshed.

'I still have your glass treasure, Alice,' a memory now prompted me to say, and I carefully extracted the green glass bauble from its safe hiding-place in the knot-hole, and handed it to her. She stood with it in the palm of her hand for a moment or two, considering it with a resentful, puzzled frown. Then she said, 'It has not changed, either. It brought you better luck than it did me, Toby—' and before I could move or protest, she laid the shining thing on my chopping-block, picked up the hammer, which she wielded with ease, and dealt the glass such a violent blow that it shivered into dust. Then she dropped the hammer, wiped her hands, and said, 'Come, let us walk.'

We left by the lane, and I told her about seeing the Frenchman's ghost, thinking, perhaps, to impress her, or to show that others, too, have had their griefs—I know not what.

But she said, indifferently, 'Oh, ghosts. Ghosts, after all, are feeble things. What can they do to us?'

'We may ourselves be ghosts one day,' I suggested.

'Not I! This one life is enough—*too much*.'

Yet she glanced with what seemed affection about the red-roofed town, as we walked along Watchbell Street, and on through Church Square, and paused above the Gun

Gardens, where the great prospect of the tidal marsh and glittering sea stretched before us. There she murmured, as if to herself, 'Yes, this place has the power to touch one's heart. Like our own house.'

'I shall never live anywhere else,' I agreed. 'Unless at Winchelsea—in Look-Out Cottage.'

At that she turned and studied me.

'What will you do, Toby? When you are grown a man?'

'I cannot marry—'

'Nor you can. I had forgotten,' she muttered, then added bitterly, 'Better such a destiny than many marriages, I daresay. How shall you make your living?'

'Oh—help my father in the brewery. I already oversee most of the accounts. John Sawnders is getting old.'

I did not tell Alice about my secret notion of becoming a literary man. I did not think she would view the plan with sympathy.

'I must go back to the brewery,' I said after a while. 'The night was very cold—I left braziers burning among the yeast tuns; but now it is growing warmer. The mash must not be allowed to work too fast.'

Alice, without comment, accompanied me into the big stone-floored place and looked with interest at the eight great oaken tubs of wort in which the barley-mash and yeast mixture was undergoing its final process before turning into beer. I—not yet having achieved my full height—was obliged to stand on two bricks to look over the rims; Alice, taller than I, needed no such aid, but walked from one tub to another, studying each in turn. The surface was frothy, in some curdled like cheese, in others wrinkled into knobs like the head of a cauliflower.

'Why are some darker than others?' she asked presently in a tone of simple interest, sounding (it occurred to me later) much more like the Alice of eight years ago.

'These are porter, made from malt that has been toasted

a dark brown. My father sells a great deal of it just now.'

'And this?'

'Small beer. Do not lean over the vat, Alice, the fumes are noxious and can be deadly.'

She moved her shoulders impatiently, but stepped away. Old Amos Fynall, the night-watchman, was there, already beginning to extinguish the braziers.

He greeted me, and I told him our sad news, that my mother had died, and Father was prostrate with grief.

'Ah, poor lady; but that'll be a blessed release to her, surelye,' he said, and looked inquiringly at Alice.

'And here's my sister Alice, Amos, returned to us; do you not remember her?'

'Lord bless me, ma'am, now I do begin to see a look of ye!' the old man exclaimed. 'Deary, deary me, 'tis a long day since ye would be begging and worriting at your dad to let ye into the brewery, and he never would. " 'Tis no place for a liddle maid," he allus said, and he'd never let ye in, no matter how ye besought him.'

'Nor he would,' said Alice slowly. 'I had forgotten that. Even my mother was not permitted to come in here.'

The thought that she was, as it were, on forbidden territory seemed to amuse her. 'Well, I am here now!' she said, and she lingered for some time, asking how the mash was made, with malted barley and hot water, at what stage the yeast and hops were added, how the beer was cleared (with isinglass, I told her) and from where we obtained our yeast and water.

The yeast, I explained, was our own plant, a leaven which my father had been propagating for years, since he found he could buy none other that fermented so well; and the water, likewise, came from our own source. Seven years ago, finding water from the town well too brackish, he had sunk his own, six fathoms deep under the brewery floor. It was fine pure water, and had never failed.

'Six fathoms!' said Alice. 'Eighty feet deep!'

'Why, Alice,' I said, 'you are a shrewd calculator,' and she gave me one of her ironic looks and said she had learned to be so during Cousin Honoria's period of affliction and infirmity, after Captain Wakehurst's death.

'Their servants were a thieving tribe, who cheated her on every hand.'

Since Alice demanded to be shown the well, old Amos took her to the inner chamber and lifted the great oaken lid, which was raised by a rope and a counter-balance.

'That never run dry!' he said proudly. 'Not even in the tarble dry summer three years agone. Don't-ee goo too near the edge now, Missy!'

The other workmen now commencing to arrive, I took Alice away, for I could see that they, like my father, did not approve of a female at large on the premises; but she cast several backward glances as we left, and, drawing a deep breath of the hop-scented air, said, 'What a pleasant way to make a living. Better at least than from the transport of slaves. I wonder that my father is not a better-tempered man.'

'He has had much to try him,' I said.

'And much of it brought on by his own fault.'

The happier turn of mind instilled in her by inspection of the brewing processes appeared to be leaving her as we walked round from the main brewery entrance into West Street; but there we encountered Hugo, just quitting my uncle's house, and he smiled at Alice, saying, 'Your grandmother wishes to see you, Cousin Alice.'

'Cousin? Are we to assume that relationship? Well, it shall be as you wish, Cousin Hugo!' and, smiling also, she followed him into Uncle Allen's house.

I re-entered Lamb House. A sentence from a long time ago had come back into my memory: Polly, saying of the

Frenchman's sweetheart 'she made away with herself, some say, by swallowing powdered glass'—and the glittering mess of dust that Alice had created when she destroyed the glass toy kept fretting my mind. Somebody should sweep it up without delay before little Jem wandered out into the yard.

But, as soon as I stepped into the hall, Agnys called to me that the Vicar wished to see me regarding the arrangements for my mother's funeral.

'Should he not see Robert?'

'Robert?' said Agnys with a sniff. 'Robert's snoring, and will be till long after noon.'

So I went round to the vicarage, and when I next visited the back yard, some other hand had swept up the glass powder.

During the ten days that succeeded Mother's death, Alice took control of the household, as she seemed well fitted to do, for she had done likewise, she said, after Captain Wakehurst's unexpected end. So, by the time of our father's recovery, Alice had established herself in a strong position. We all greatly missed my grandmother, still bedridden, but it became plain that her broken hip joint was not likely to mend well, and, indeed, after this time she gradually faded away. Alice, meanwhile, had made herself indispensable at Lamb House.

My father did not like it; he became ever more silent and withdrawn; I would catch him sometimes staring at Alice (as he had used to at me) as if he could scarcely endure the sight of her. But he said nothing. Her activities, at least, created comfort and order, and a well-run household; whereas those of Robert, after my mother's death, proceeded from one fearful excess to another—drinking, dicing, attending cock-fights; on one occasion he was caught passing counterfeit coin at a low alehouse outside Playden; my father was in a continual state of apprehension as to what Robert would do next, and several times threatened to turn him out of doors.

It was inevitable, I can see, that Hugo should fall in love with Alice. And she appeared to reciprocate. With the rest of us she was angry, and would remain so. We had been happy, fortunate, and thriving, all the time that she was bitterly unhappy; and she could never forget that fact, nor allow me, at any rate, to forget it.

But Hugo did not lie under that shadow. It was plain that, for Hugo, Alice was some kind of angelic being. In his eyes she was surpassingly beautiful, and—under his eyes—she became so. She was the first female he had ever looked at (for he took no interest in the young ladies of Rye) and to him she appeared enveloped in heavenly radiance.

'Why did you never describe her properly, Toby?' he said, over and over. 'You told me she was a fat little dumpy creature. But she is so beautiful! She is like a burning torch!' And he went on for ever in that vein—she was a candle, a taper, a tigress, a burning bush, a shaft of firelight.

'Toby, can you not talk some sense into Hugo's head?' Uncle Allen said to me privily. 'He is quite besotted about your sister! For three weeks he has not opened a single book. And Ellis had said that Dr Milliken was so delighted with Hugo—thought him so full of promise—they both have such high hopes for him—'

When I asked Hugo how the interview with his tutor had prospered, I received only a vague, scant reply—'Oh, Cambridge—! I do not know, now, if I can be bothered to go up. Three years out of a man's life—and for what? A dull paper qualification. Cambridge is a mere grind—reading books which I may just as well read at home. I do not wish to leave Rye now that your sister has come.'

And Alice? What did she really think of Hugo? How could I tell? Most certainly it pleased her, made her happy to be so worshipped. And more especially so, no doubt, after the terrible usage she had received at our cousin's. But did she love Hugo? I had no means of knowing.

Hugo was a well-enough-looking fellow by then: not handsome, but with a great quality of directness and sincerity in his countenance which made it attractive; he had his mop of yellow hair still, bright as ever, and fine white teeth which showed often in a ready smile; he had, at all times, a look of intelligence, as well as a frank, lively manner. Through all his growing he remained thin and lanky, but had shot up in the last year, so that he overtopped even my brother Robert by several inches. And he dressed well; not in a dandified style, but with neatness and elegance. All this, I could see, my sister Alice enjoyed; she liked to be with him, to walk and talk and laugh with him; she enjoyed parading with him through Rye, along Market Street, around Church Square. Walking, laughing with him seemed to repay a small portion of the childhood that had been stolen from her.

If she were aware of the gossip that ran rife through Rye concerning her—'*What can* have befallen that Alice Lamb—she has come home resembling a Death's Head, they must have used her monstrous ill—brought on a fatal convulsion in her poor mother, it's said—looks no better than she should be!—passing strange those Wakehursts never found a husband for her?—twenty now, if she's a day, past marriageable age—' all of which gossip was furiously repeated to me by Agnys and Polly—if she were aware of this, Alice paid it no heed whatsoever. To walk abroad with Hugo, gay and uncaring, was her reply.

And the day came when she said to my father, after dinner, 'Hugo and I wish to get married, Papa.'

My father, predictably, flew into a rage. Any threat of

a change that disturbed his tranquillity had this effect on him. But, by degrees, Alice talked him round.

'After all, I am sure you would not wish to have me remain here in the house for the remainder of my life.'

'Who will take care of the housekeeping if you go?' he demanded, most unreasonably, since he could not have depended upon her being there to take up the task at my mother's death.

'Sophy will, I suppose. But that is of no concern to me. I don't propose to be your housekeeper for ever,' Alice said coolly.

'How dare you speak so, miss?'

'Well, Father; if you object to my marrying Hugo, I will be very happy, instead, to run your brewery for you. I should enjoy such an occupation, and would do it far better than Robert, or Toby, who, doubtless, is dutiful enough, but his heart is not in it. He has higher wishes.' Alice shot me a cold look.

'Run the *brewery*? Are you out of your mind, girl?' Father's face was working like one of his own yeast-brews. 'How could a *woman* run a *business*?'

'No; well; I guessed that is the way you would reply. Luckily Hugo will have a comfortable fortune of his own in four years. His trustees might release it sooner, if they approve his marriage. Therefore if you, Father, will give me some kind of dowry, and if you can persuade Uncle Allen to sanction the match, we shall manage tolerably enough. And if not—we can always go and live in Look-Out Cottage,' Alice finished, with a small, sour smile.

All my father would say was, 'Time. Give me time. I will see. I will think it over.'

After Alice had quitted the room (to report to Hugo, no doubt) I said, 'Father, you cannot permit this marriage.'

He stared at me as if one of the spoons had started to talk.

'*Toby*? What affair is it of yours, pray?'

'It is my business,' I said. 'Alice is my sister. Once I loved her dearly. Hugo is my friend. She is nearly three years the elder of the pair—that is bad in itself. But, much worse than that, I do not believe that, in her heart, she loves him at all. She is merely making a convenience of him.'

'That is his concern,' said my father. 'Or your Uncle Allen's. Hugo is no responsibility of mine.'

'Father! You know the match would be disgraceful—scandalous! Hugo is only a boy, he has no experience of life or—or women. He has never lived anywhere but here in Rye, he has seen nothing of the world.'

'He has seen India,' argued my father.

'That was when he was eight! All his career is still before him. He is clever, he could be a scholar—Mr Ellis said Dr Milliken thought very highly of him. To throw all that aside at the first—'

My throat closed, I came to a stop.

'None of that is of any moment to me,' said my father, who, true to his nature, became more fixed in obstinacy, the more arguments were raised against him.

'Listen, Father,' said I, growing desperate, 'You know, you *must* know the real impediment to this marriage. You must, surely, be aware of what happened to Alice during the years that she lived with those—those Wakehursts?' I stared at him, and he stared, with a fixed and marble countenance, back at me. 'Alice is not a proper person to marry Hugo!' I said in a trembling voice.

'I have no idea what you are talking about,' said my father. He raised a hand, before I could reply, and went on, 'Nor is this a subject at all suitable for *your* lips, Toby. I am surprised at you—I am indeed. And deeply shocked. You seem to be making some atrocious accusation against your sister, which—which should not be uttered by any right-thinking person. Let alone her brother! Let alone a boy of your age! You should be ashamed of yourself.

Especially since she is not here to speak in her own defence.'

'Send for her, then!'

'Be silent, Toby. I will not listen to you.'

'But if the aspersions are true?' I said hoarsely.

My father's answer was to leave the room.

I then appealed to my Uncle Allen—not speaking so plainly as I had to my father, but saying, with truth, that I did not think Alice could or would make Hugo happy, that I believed such a marriage would be a disaster.

'She behaves kindly now, and smiles on him, because he so dotes on her—which has never happened to her before; but that will come to an end, he will resume his interest in his old pursuits, and that will offend Alice and make her angry, and then she will be bitterly unkind to him.'

'Toby, I do believe you,' said Uncle Allen. 'I fear you are right. But what can I do? I am not in reality Hugo's guardian, only his godfather, I can only advise him, I have no legal power over him. His trustees are simply concerned with his fortune. In four years he will be a rich man. He can, in the meantime, if necessary, borrow on those expectations. If he chooses to do this, I cannot stop him, if your father sees no impediment to the marriage and will not act in the matter.'

But my father, it was plain, daily became more reconciled to the match. It would see Alice respectably off his hands; doing, even, quite well for herself. And once she was married the gossip that buzzed around Rye would begin to abate.

I then tried talking to Hugo, but he was in a queer, edgy, unapproachable mood.

'Why are you no longer my friend, Toby? Why are you behaving like a dog-in-the-manger? I used to think I knew and loved you better than anybody else in the world, but now I can't understand you.—For instance, do you know what Alice told me? She said that once you saw a ghost, in Lamb House garden! Why did you never tell *me* that? You saw a ghost, in your own garden, and never told me!'

'For heaven's sake, Hugo! It was of no importance. It was years ago—before you ever came to Rye. Why raise that now?'

'Because it is important. *Why* did you never tell me about it?' he persisted childishly.

'I—I—it is hard to express.' I was fumbling, taken off guard, being beset, just at that time, with so many cares that seemed weightier. 'I suppose—it just seemed a private thing, a kind of family phantom. Dear Hugo, what *can* it matter? But this engagement between you and Alice—it seems so hasty, so ill-judged—can you not at least wait to marry a year or two—until you have looked about you—if only until you have taken your degree?'

Ignoring this completely, Hugo said, 'A family phantom. That is it! You are not prepared to accept *me* in your precious Lamb family. I am not good enough for your sister! You seem to have forgotten that I am your blood brother. Do you no longer remember the oath that we swore?'

I stared at Hugo in consternation. For I had, I was obliged to admit, wholly forgotten that boyish oath, sworn when we were so much younger.

'You don't wish to share your sister with me! And another thing: you never told me that she had written you a letter! After Moses died! I had to learn that from her, also. I suppose that was of no importance either? Like the ghost? What other secrets have you been keeping from me, Toby?'

'Hugo, the ghost was only a—a kind of vision. An illusion, most likely. Seen for two seconds, no longer.'

'And never shared, in the course of eight years' friendship?' I had never seen Hugo so angry, so bitterly hurt. He seemed like a stranger. 'You resemble your father, Toby,' he said, biting off his words. 'You are a miser.'

'Very well—have it your own way—I am a miser!' Cut to the quick, I turned and left him, without asking, as I had meant, how much Alice had revealed to him (if anything) about her life in Tunbridge Wells. And I did not see him again. In the end, Uncle Allen did manage to prevail upon him to go up to Cambridge, at least for one term. If Hugo would agree to this, Allen said, he, Allen, would use his influence to induce Hugo's trustees to advance him some part of his inheritance at Christmastime.

So Hugo left Rye, not unwilling, perhaps, in his heart, to get at least a glimpse of the new world that Cambridge had to offer. He went off without saying goodbye to me, and I missed him with every breath; it was the first time, since his arrival, that we had been parted for longer than ten days. And the thought that we had parted as unfriends was worst of all.

Alice blamed me for his going.

'You are simply jealous, because I took your friend!' she flamed at me. 'And so you spoke against me to Allen. You envied our happiness. During all the years when you used to write to me "Hugo and I did this, Hugo and I are doing that, Hugo and I . . ." how do you think *I* felt then? Situated as I was? While you never spared a thought for me—?'

'Alice, I *did* think. I had *not* forgotten you. I wrote—I kept on writing—'

'But now,' she went on as if I had not spoken, 'the boot is on the other foot. So, Master Toby, you must just make the best of matters. You may—' and she gave me a knifelike glance 'you may, if you like, be godfather to our first boy. Since you will have none of your own.'

'*Alice!*'

'You are our enemy, Toby! I know it was you who

worked on Uncle Allen to persuade Hugo to go to Cambridge. But he will come back to me,' she said with certainty. 'He will come back, I know.'

'Alice,' I said, 'did you ever tell Hugo the—the story that you told me?'

'No,' she said. 'I did not. And I don't intend to. Why should I? It is the past now. It has nothing to do with our life ahead. Men, when they marry, do not tell their wives of their past lives. Captain Wakehurst did not tell Honoria—'

'But, Alice, you *must* tell Hugo. You are entirely other than what he thinks. How can you possibly deceive him so?'

She gave me a look of real ferocity.

'So, injustice is to follow me always? Is that it? Because I have been wickedly misused in my childhood, is that to cut me off from happiness for the rest of my life?'

'Alice, you are not what Hugo believes you to be. You are cheating him. Can't you stop thinking about yourself, and consider what you owe to Hugo?'

'I owe him nothing,' said Alice. 'I owe nothing to anybody in the world. All the luck I can get is owing to me—and I intend to see that it is paid! You are a turncoat, Toby. Once you loved me above all others, but now you grudge us our future—just because you yourself can never marry.'

This was so wholly untrue, so wide of the mark—since I had not the least wish to marry—that it left me speechless, and, seeing that I could get nowhere by argument or persuasion, I went away and unburdened myself to the Vicar, who listened to me gravely.

'Well, Toby,' he said at last, 'you have a hard problem there, and I am very sorry for you. Since your father says that he will not act in the matter . . . Have you prayed to God about it?'

'Yes, sir, most vehemently.'

'Hugo should know all the facts of the case, certainly,' he said. 'I think the only thing left is for you to write to Hugo. Write him a letter. It will be painful for you, it will go against the grain; but that is your duty. He should know what she has been, before he commits himself for ever.'

So, that is what I did. I wrote to Hugo. Feeling a traitor to him, to myself, to Alice, even to God.

I wrote to him, but never received an answer to my letter. Like those to Alice, it seemed to vanish into a void.

I know he received it, though, because of the sequel.

Three weeks later Agnys roused me, at half-past four one morning, to ask in perturbation,

'Do ye know where Miss Alice can be, Master Toby? Her bed's not been slept in. Nor the children haven't seen her—nor Polly—nor Dickie, but he says a letter came for her, yester-eve, which he gave her—'

A dreadful fear seized me.

'Alice had a letter? Where from?'

'How should I know, Master Toby?' said Agnys, who had never learned to read.

I ran up to Alice's chamber and looked about. The handsome, tawdry clothes hung on their pegs, the bed was smooth, nothing out of place.

My father still slept, in the King's Room. I went down, searched in the dining-room, the parlour, the little office, looking on to West Street, where Alice and Hugo had first met. There I saw a square white paper on the mantelshelf, with TOBY written on it.

I picked it up as if it were a snake about to bite me.

'Dear Brother,' said the writing inside. 'This is the second letter I send you, and the last. Because of what you told Hugo, all is at an end between us. He is in a rage because, he says, he can't endure things being kept from him. He says if I had told him my history he would have accepted it and me, but now it is too late. He says you and I are secretive and deceitful, and deceit is what he can't abide. So, Toby, I hope you are satisfied. My life, that was like to have been mended, is broke again. It is not my intention to stay and keep house in a place that is home no more. Tell my father I would gladly have worked in his business, and if his next brew is too bitter for the customers, he has only himself to thank. And you, Toby, will never forget me. ALICE.'

Dear God, I thought, the brewery! I ran there, through the black dawn. A storm of wind and rain had blown all night, and daylight would be slow in coming.

On the way up the lane I passed somebody, a man, but the light was too bad to see more than his outline.

In the brew-hall I found old Amos, quietly plodding among the vats, with a rush-light, scraping off the foam with a paddle when it threatened to bubble over.

'Is—is all well, Amos?' I stammered.

'Why, yes, Master Toby,' he said, seeming surprised to see me. 'Naught amiss here. All's quiet. 'Tis a cold old night, but I've known colder—' and he was rambling on, pleased to have company, when I interrupted him.

'Did Miss Alice come here?'

'Ah! That she did, Master Toby. An hour agone. Told me Polly had a message for me in the kitchen. But I rackon she was mistook, for when I went, 'twas no such thing.'

'And when you came back she was not here?'

'Why, no, Master Toby, she warn't—' but now there was a note of anxiety in his voice.

I had begun hurrying from one vat to another, looking to see if the surface had been disturbed. But all appeared normal enough. Besides, how could Alice ever climb into one of those great vessels, higher than my head?

Amos, beginning to pick up the infection of my fear, limped after me, mumbling, 'What is it, then, Master Toby? What do-ee think she've been and done? She wouldn't goo a-meddling with the wort, surelye? Not Miss Alice?'

A worse dread came to me, and I ran through into the storage vault, where the great six-hundred-gallon hogsheads of porter stood slowly maturing, and where the well was located.

Its massive oaken lid had been drawn back by the counter-balance, and remained tilted.

'That's a puzzle,' said old Amos. 'How did the lid get opened up then?'

But I knew that we need look no further for Alice. She was down below, six fathoms down . . .

Late that night, when all was over, I thought of the man I had passed in the lane, and remembered his outline. His cape had been flung up across his shoulder, and he passed me with his head turned the other way, as if my affairs were no concern of his.

It is too late now, I thought. Too late to tell Hugo about him.

Hugo never found occasion to return to Rye. He remained at Cambridge, studied with distinction, became a Fellow, then went abroad, back to India, where his parents had lived. I heard that he made something of a name for himself, as a historian and geographer. He also indited one work of fiction, early in his career, entitled *The Heart of Stone*. That I did take pains to acquire and peruse, and it caused me some pain, for it seemed a travesty of various events which I recalled in a very different light. Also, I must acknowledge, I did not consider it particularly well written.

My Uncle Allen missed Hugo sadly at first, but returned to his solitary ways, after the death of my grandmother. The year after Hugo went up to Cambridge he was elected Mayor of Rye for the fourth time.

My father, after Alice's death, became, for several years, subject to acute headaches and confusion of memory. During that period my brother Jem and I looked after the brewery between us. (My brother Robert had died of a syncope after a violent drinking bout in 1736.) In 1741 I had the honour to be elected a Freeman of the town of Rye, and my brother Jem was, likewise, in 1742. After some years my father had recovered from his symptoms, and feelings of oppression and unworthiness. But the murder of Uncle Allen, also in 1742, caused a relapse. The fact that Allen had been stabbed *in mistake for my father* was enough to overset the latter's frail balance once more. (This murder has been sufficiently recorded elsewhere, so I will only allude to it briefly.) The crime was committed by Breads, a demented and drunken butcher, who had had a long-standing dispute with my father about the size of his bill, and who made not the least secret of his culpability.—When my father, pronouncing sentence from the bench of magistrates, asked the wretch if he had anything to say for himself, Breads roared out, pointing at my father: '*That's* the man I meant it for, and I'd kill him now if I could!' The body of Breads, after hanging, was set up beside the high road from Rye to Winchelsea, as the wife-murderer Robinson had been, two hundred years earlier.

Needless to say, it took my father some months to rally after this shocking event. It may be worth recording that, on the night of the murder, my dear mother, then dead for some years, appeared to my father in a dream, weeping and wringing her hands, and warning him that her beloved brother was in grave danger.

There is little else to relate. My lameness, in later years, returned to plague me, and became almost as acute as when I was a child. The Frenchman's prophecy was fulfilled, insofar as that I never achieved my wish to become an author; this chronicle (which I have completed for my own satisfaction) being the longest piece of writing I ever undertook. When it is done I shall amuse myself by laying it by, in a little secret closet I have had constructed in the west bedroom, once Alice's, now my study and chamber (Jem and his brood occupying the rest of the house). I could not, would not, dare not publish such a history now. The events it records are too terrible, too recent, the people concerned are too well known to all our neighbours and kindred. But—as a wound requires purefying, as a fetid room demands the blessing and ventilation of God's cleansing wind—so this grief demands to be told, demands to be heard. And I pray, I beseech that some kindly hand will, in years to come, rescue our tale from its hiding-place and bring it before the impartial eyes of posterity.

My life has been long, but hollow. I am Mayor of Rye in the year in which I write, 1784, but that is no particular satisfaction. I think most fondly of the early days, fifty years ago, when Hugo and I explored Rye together, or drove in our pony-trap to the bluebell woods.

I recall Hugo saying, on one occasion, 'What are we, Toby, indeed? Perhaps we are nothing but the raw material of a ghost story.'

Who will publish that story, I wonder?

The Shade in the Alley

2 · HENRY

through all his works with the splendour of a royal progress. He knew these places, he could describe them, he had
been there for glittering weekend parties!

(Yet, we wonder now, had he *quite* caught the authentic
nomenclature in some of those cases?—do Fawns, Bounds,
and Branches ring absolutely true? Or do they have a faintly synthetic air, uneasily hovering in the suburban vicinity
of Mon Repos and Dunroamin?)

Such mansions, whether real or fictional, necessarily
coloured his view of Lamb House. When he referred
to its 'inconspicuous little charm' was our friend, in
his mind's eye, comparing it with Chatsworth, Wilton,
Cliveden? Or did he show just a touch of hypocrisy in his
almost deprecating attitude to a domicile which could, in
all truth, compare very favourably indeed with Dr Sloper's
handsome residence in Washington Square?

If the house felt any affront, it, at that time, made no sign.

To furnish his twelve rooms with dignity he would
require additional funds—since he did not, as yet, propose
too severely to despoil De Vere Gardens, which would
remain, for the moment, his London pied-à-terre. 'I have
bought two maps, five prints, and a chest of drawers,' he
wrote. Plain green drugget covered the wide stairs. Mrs
Warren had already promised that she would take care of
the curtains.

A new novel, *The Awkward Age*, had for some time
been projected and was now taking form in his mind;
but in the meantime a shorter work for *Collier's* maga-
zine would help provide 'some good mahogany and brass,
some Chippendale and Sheraton, a little faded tapestry'.
He planned a story—'a little book' he termed it—of two
children misused, unhappily permitted to share evil secrets
of adult life—two children isolated in a venerable country
mansion. Edward White Benson, the Archbishop of Canterbury, had, a couple of years previously, presented him

with the germ of the idea: a tale, or rather a mere snatch, a fragment concerning children who had, by a pair of demon spirits, been lured to destruction.

But why should *this* particular story float to the surface of the writer's mind so promptly after his having signed the lease of Lamb House? Could he, already, have had any feeling, any message about the children who had lived there in a previous epoch? Had he, conceivably, heard the legend of the Frenchman in the garden? Did he, inspecting empty parlours where paper was to be peeled from fine old panelling, upstairs rooms where builders were at work on improvements to antiquated sanitary arrangements—did he, looking out through the pleasant french door of the dining-room, imagine that he could discern some excluded, menacing figure—such as Peter Quint—looking in?

Our writer gave no overt indication of any such super-natural influence. *The Turn of the Screw* was completed, and duly published in *Collier's*, from January to April 1899. In June the move to Lamb House was accomplished, and, almost at once, the hardly-ceasing procession of guests began to make their appearance. Oliver Wendell Holmes, Mrs Fields, Sarah Orne Jewett, the Bourgets, the Curtises, Edward Warren, the Gosses, Howard Sturgis, and, in October, when the summer spate was diminishing, Jonathan Sturgis, who stayed for two months.

'I wish I could give you a picture of this little red, pointed, almost medieval town with its sea wall and its Norman relic of Ypres Castle which they call here "Wipers"—perched on a hill in the midst of the grey-green sand coloured waste of Romney Marsh, an Anglo-Saxon Mont St Michel, long deserted by the sea, yet with the colour and scent of the sea in its quiet brown streets . . .' wrote Jonathan to William Fullerton.

Jonathan was a sensitive guest, who did not impinge on his host's working hours in the Garden Room but, guest house.—Fortunately no great harm ensued; but the mischance may illustrate as well, perhaps, the slight discord between guest and host, for Paul Bourget maintained a strongly Catholic and conservative attitude relating to the Dreyfus case, whereas our friend, with equal strength, upheld the opposing view.

'I have been here a week and depart tomorrow or next day. It has been rather a tension,' he wrote his brother William, after extolling the beauties and amenities of the mountainside estate, adding, 'poor dear little Lamb House veils its face with humility and misery.' Nonetheless, he confessed, he was homesick. 'Never again will I leave it!'

He travelled on to Genoa and to Venice (pausing there to write a story for Lady Randolph Churchill). Then to Rome, where he met and fell in love with the handsome Norwegian-American young sculptor Hendrik Andersen, and impulsively purchased one of his *oeuvres*, a small terra-cotta bust. 'I shall put it in the dining-room at Lamb House,' he said, inviting the sculptor to come and visit him there. Then on to Capri, Vallombrosa, Florence—where there occurred a slight earthquake. By now Europe was dusty and displeasing, in summer heat. On the 7th of July our traveller might be found eagerly re-crossing the Channel to the home port of Folkestone. He had been absent from Rye and Lamb House for almost four months. 'Oh, it is a joy to be once more in this refreshed and renovated refuge!' he wrote, happily re-ensconced in repainted Lamb House with its green garden. There, too, waiting for him in his locked desk drawer, lay the rescued manuscript.

Yet, strangely perhaps, he did not at once take it out and peruse it. First the bust of Alberto Bevilacqua, which had arrived in its crate, must be carefully unpacked and established in a place of honour in the dining-room niche; then, shortly after, appeared the handsome sculptor himself. A slight misunderstanding was soon resolved:

at the end of the day, brought his friend up to date with London and New York literary and society news.

In the Cage had been finished after the move to Lamb House, and by now *The Awkward Age* was well under way—another story about young people's exposure to the hateful secrets of the adult world. At this time the Spanish-American war and the Dreyfus case were peripheral anxieties, distant troubles that did no more than faintly ruffle the coastal waters of our writer's tranquil inland sea. Lamb House remained quiet, biding its time; it had, after all, another fifteen years in which to utter its message. At present it enfolded its tenant in the warmth of an embrace—whether conjugal, fraternal, or maternal, the recipient might have been hard put to it to say. *The Great Good Place* was written, with evident relish, *The Awkward Age* completed. Our friend had an enviable ability to move back and forth, in composition, between a major and a minor work, to the enrichment of both.

The house remained quiet.

Then, in 1899, it made its first move, late one evening, while the householder worked at his desk (the domestic retinue long abed) at correcting the galleys of *The Awkward Age*, in the upstairs study that had come to be called the Green Room. 'The wind booms in the old chimneys, wails and shrieks about the old walls. I sit, however, in the little warm white study . . . and the divine unrest again touches me.' He was in fact planning a trip to Italy, during which he hoped to gestate the idea for 'some strong short novel' and to return with it 'all figured out'.

But now as, having at last completed the galleys, he indited a few final notes and sorted his personal papers preparatory to departure, he was disconcerted to observe small spirals of sharply acidic blue woodsmoke beginning to creep from between the floorboards of the little warm white study and to fill the air with a sinister haze. And the little study, surely, was growing even warmer than he had a right to expect?

Dismayed, he roused the servants, the alcoholic Smiths who slept on the floor above (their alcoholism as yet within bounds). Smith hacked up two floorboards near the corner fireplace, and a dense cloud of smoke burst out: a whole beam, under the floor, was gently, wickedly smouldering. Pails of water and soaked sponges served to quench it, but not for long; at 2.45 in the morning the master, still at his correspondence, perceived, with affright, tongues of flame shooting from the hole, and woke the servants yet again. Now the fire brigade had to be summoned; the firemen were obliged to break through the dining-room wall and ceiling in order to attack the source of the blaze.

Could this have been a cry for help from the house? Or was it, like a slighted wife, piqued at our friend's apologetic reference to its 'inconspicuous little charm', wreaking a childish revenge?

Despite this minor calamity the owner took his pre-arranged departure for the Continent early in March, and spent a fortnight in Paris, where he received word from Edward Warren as to the repairs that were being put in hand. The dining-room fireplace and chimney must be rebuilt; it was there that the mischief had originated. Scorched paint and smokestains would be replaced and repaired. All would be complete by the, as yet undecided, date of the master's return.

But now arrived a wholly unexpected bulletin from Warren: a document, a manuscript, consisting of a quantity of handwritten pages, somewhat smokestained, but still legible, had been discovered in a small concealed niche or cupboard, laid open in the wall of the Green Room during the necessary joiners' work. The MS appeared to be some kind of a journal. What, inquired Warren, did his friend

wish to be done with this find, which, as it came t on his property, must be adjudged as belonging to l least for the present, under the terms of the lease?

'Consult Bellingham,' our friend telegraphed in He was just about to set out southward for Le Pl Paul Bourget's villa near Hyeres. Arrived there, he re Warren's reply. The Bellinghams were not at all int ed in an old, smoke-stained, handwritten journal; if tenant wished to keep it, he was welcome to make whatever use he chose. The latter accordingly sent in: tions to Warren to have the papers, for the time, l away safely in a drawer of his desk in the now-res study; he would, at leisure, after his return home, rea document and appraise it. 'Do not think of entrusting the mails,' he wrote with practical good sense. 'It can v little longer, as it has waited so long.' Nevertheless, ne such a discovery could not but stir him strangely. Ten before, in *The Aspern Papers*, he had written abou fearsome importance, almost diabolical in their pow influence human actions, of ancient love-letters, treas as sacred relics, fiercely coveted, vindictively destro And then, by odd coincidence, five years later, in a entitled *Sir Dominic Ferrand*, he had told of a *trouv* papers, concealed in a second-hand desk, which w mysteriously affect the life of their finder.

Was history about to repeat itself? Would his life be given a similar twist?

What kind of chronicle or dossier would this that awaited him at Rye? Whose long-forgotten g triumphs, crimes, or trivial acts lay there revealed?

In his preoccupation with this news—possibly legacy of disturbance from the small drama at Rye also instrumental—he committed a curious, a mos characteristic blunder: normally so neat, so carefu considerate, he set fire to the curtains of Paul Bou

Andersen had thought, hoped, that our friend planned to write a laudatory article about him in some English journal; he was soon disabused of this notion.—But his bust, in the dining-room, he was assured, would be certain to have many and celebrated admirers. The visit proved to be brief—three days only—but it had a profound, disquieting impact on the host. 'I was absurdly sorry to lose you when, that afternoon of last month, we walked sadly to the innocent and kindly little station together . . . I walked up from the station, that soft summer morning of your departure, much more lonely than I should have thought . . . I miss you—keep on doing so—out of all proportion to the too few hours you were here . . . your poor, helpless, far-off but all devoted H.J.'

The letters, the grief, the note of authentic love, would continue for years, unassuaged.

Somehow at this precise juncture our poor friend, lonely, forlorn as he was, caught up in the emotional turmoil resulting from Hendrik's visit, could not find in himself the necessary interest or spirit to disinter the sooty manuscript from its second tomb in his desk drawer, and apply himself to reading it.—Let it remain where it was with all it might hold of complication or responsibility; let it remain in the drawer a few weeks longer. So he procrastinated.

But now two other agitating and unforeseen sets of tidings came to shatter his peace of mind. William was ill: William the elder brother, whom he had not seen for seven years, had been diagnosed as suffering from a serious valvular lesion; William was about to set sail from New England to take a cure in Germany, at Bad Nauheim.

And Bellingham, the owner and landlord of Lamb House, had died, his widow did not want the house, his son was setting forth to make a fortune in the Klondyke (where the poor fellow was to die untimely) and the property was offered for sale to the sitting tenant at the price of £2,000 or $10,000.

Always, in the past, the younger brother had been overshadowed, through childhood and adolescence, by his active, intelligent, achieving elder, who was removed from him in age only by fifteen months but who, due to his very different temperament, was the friend of 'boys who liked to curse and swear', boys who called the younger brother 'sissy' because of his proclivity for reading. Throughout all of his fiction our writer had gone out of his way to indulge younger brothers and to dispose, sometimes quite summarily, of older ones. Only too clearly did he recall those days when William went roistering off and engaged in adventures while his cadet sat in the window-seat and read Leslie's *Life of Constable*. And how, later, in his teens, he had come to understand that, only when William was away from home, could he himself enjoy full health and muster enough energy to establish himself successfully by writing; as soon as his older brother returned, the mysterious afflictions—back pain, languor and depression—would also return to plague him. The two brothers could not, it seemed, both be at home and both be healthy at the same time. If one throve, the other sickened.—Indeed there was a firm family theory that illness shifted from one member to another, that one member's success was balanced by another's failure.

Then, beyond all this, there lay William's attitude to our friend's writing: overtly encouraging, yet the older brother so very often contrived to damn, in his critical comments—the stories were 'too thin', the style far too complicated, the characters in the plays spent far too much time explaining themselves. That there was a grain of truth in some of these points made them no easier to bear. This bombardment of criticism had continued, and *would* continue, throughout both their lives, long after the younger had publicly been acknowledged a master of his craft: 'Won't you, just to please Brother, sit down and write a new book with no twilight or mustiness in the plot?' begged William after reading *The Golden Bowl*; and his junior was stung, for once, into retort: 'Let me say, dear William, that I shall be greatly humiliated if you *do* like it . . .'

In William's company, though, invariably, our friend became mild and conciliating, returned always to the humble younger brother status; between them, sibling rivalry had never been admitted, and the affection between them was warm and genuine. William's grave illness now created a terror in our hero: his own life seemed threatened, he began miserably to worry about his own heart.

Yet at the same time—without pausing to wonder whether William, in such a precarious state of health, was in a fit condition to be troubled by business questions—the younger brother sent off to him an agitated letter of ten pages, marshalling all the arguments in favour of the purchase of Lamb House—but also, it appeared, asking his advice in the matter. William, ailing and low-spirited, replied that the price seemed very extravagant—which evoked, at once, an indignant outcry from England: 'I do, strange as it may appear to you, in this matter, know more or less what I'm about . . .'

Without further ado, in August 1899, our friend bought the house on a mortgage; he found that, in fact, he needed a smaller capital outlay than he had feared. And, in October, William, somewhat recovered, left Germany for a visit to Rye, with his wife Alice and daughter Peggy.

William, accustomed to the amplitude and space, indoors and out, of New England living, found Lamb House, which he now entered for the first time, rather small and cramped; indeed he found Rye itself tiny and claustrophobic.

'One wonders how *families* ever could have been reared in most of the houses,' he wrote. Lamb House he found 'all very simple and on a small scale'. His illness grew worse again; he suffered a sharp attack of chest pains and had to be hurried up to London to stay at De Vere Gardens and consult a heart specialist, who ordered him down to Malvern for the waters. In December, however, the William James family would be able to return to Rye, where the new owner of Lamb House—alarmed, harassed, perturbed by these anxieties (he described William's visit as 'a tension of the keenest—a strain of the sorest') these various to-ings and fro-ings, had been unable to settle to a sustained piece of work. Instead, so as to raise immediate funds, he had written a number of short stories.

And he had, at last, found in himself the will and impetus to remove the yellow, smoke-stained, dog-eared manuscript from its hiding-place, and to read it.

For now, after all, along with the house, it might truly be said to belong to him.

The deciphering and absorption of Toby Lamb's journal had been a process that occupied our friend for a number of wintry November evenings. The writing was faint and crabbed, the paper dingy and stained. Arriving, finally, at the *finis*, turning the ultimate page, the reader found himself in a singular condition of trance, almost of suspended animation. A need still further to postpone the return to his normal intellectual state kept him for a further indefinite period, holding, as it were, his mental breath. So many questions loomed unanswered beyond the gates of conscious knowledge; so many never *would* be answered. For as long as might be, he deferred making any decision about the thing.

Reading the script had been, in itself, an interesting respite from his own, at present, somewhat acutely sensitive consciousness; this relief he could not fail to acknowledge. Soon, of course (indeed already it had taken place at a lower level of internal process, his own peculiar powerful function had acted by itself even as he read) that formidable critical faculty was engaged, which must always come into play, leaving no book, no story, no single sentence unchallenged, and by which his friends and colleagues were continually irked when, presenting their most recent works for approval, they found themselves deluged with torrents of measured criticism and suggestions for improvement, instead of the unstinted praise which is all that any writer, on such an occasion, ever hopes to receive. Toby's journal could be, our friend had, from the start, divined, so much *more* remarkable, so much finer, if only the poor dear boy had specified more, localised more, and, after writing once, had recomposed and reconstructed; it might have become, who knows, a small masterpiece, if various amendments had been made to it which instantly flashed into our writer's apperception as, making his careful way through the document, he 'took it in'. His fingers itched to snatch up a pen and start at once on the emendations. He had said once that he was a wretched person to read a novel: 'I begin so quick and concomitantly, for myself, to write it . . .' Of course it may have been true, probably was, that young Toby had written it mainly for himself, but after all, the unfortunate boy had wished to become a writer. His little piece could have furnished a small valuable insight, a real window on the past. (Our friend could not, he found, avoid thinking of Toby as a boy, though, in fact, he had lived on into middle age). And there was *one* signal and specific change which would, straight away, effect a marked improvement, would strengthen and dignify the little narrative, 'open it' so to speak, wider, and give it greater depth . . .

Then, running parallel to these critical awarenesses, flowed a wonderful, a truly striking sense of astonishment, of recognition. For so very many elements of Toby's tale meshed themselves with our reader's own personal experience and seemed to cry out to him with a strange, piercing familiarity! Toby, like himself, had been a younger brother; Toby, like himself, had been crippled, afflicted by an accident in a fire; had been unable to play his part in full-fledged masculine life.—Yet Toby, it seemed, assisted and healed by the powerful golden benediction of friendship, had succeeded in battling against his disability, almost in vanquishing it; only to have it return in later life. Toby, like our friend, had a beloved sister Alice—and here the correspondence between the two lives became even more poignant. For Toby's Alice, unlike Henry's, had not remained at home, but had been catapulted at an early age into the adult world, and had suffered incapacitating wounds. Which fate had been worse? our friend wondered painfully. *What* precise vile treatment had been meted out to Alice Lamb, he shrank from contemplating. (And here, he must acknowledge, Toby Lamb had exercised a true writer's judgment. 'So long as the events are veiled the imagination will run riot and depict all sorts of horrors, but as soon as the veil is lifted, all mystery disappears and with it the sense of terror,' our friend once acutely remarked, discussing what he called his process of adumbration.) Well, Toby had not lifted any veil, and our reader, at liberty to imagine all sorts of horrors, much preferred to avert his mind. But the horrors that had assailed his own Alice, poor Alice James, he *did* know—only too well—the suffocating sense of loss, of waste, the mental misery which made, in the end, actual palpable physical disease appear in the guise of a friendly rescuer.

'I feel the unholy granite substance in my breast,' Alice James announced triumphantly, and welcomed the cancer in the manner of a soldier who views with elation the medal pinned on his uniform, as evidence of valour in combat, and evidence, also, that the combat is finally over and done.

Which fate had been worse? our reader wondered again. Alice Lamb might have been able to redeem herself in time, if she had been given the chance; she would have liked to manage her father's brewery; but Alice James had never been given the chance to manage anything. Even her letters, unlike those of her busy brothers, had not been considered worth preservation. Doubtless they related little of interest—what, after all, had she to communicate, save her own restless, devouring thoughts? 'When one can only take a passive part in life, the base, crude blankness of nature here with nothing to call one out of one's self plays upon the soul and makes the process of getting well a task and not a pleasure . . .' she recorded. 'The fact is, I have been dead so long, and it has been simply such a grim shoving of the hours behind me . . . that now it's only the shrivelling of an empty pea pod that has to be completed.'

Could words more painful than these ever be written? Her brother doubted it.

The story of Alice Lamb had most excruciatingly revived in him echoes of the story of Alice James, who, only seven years ago, had died in London and been cremated at Woking—died at the early age of forty-two after enduring half a lifetime of illness and frustration.

Then there was the story of Toby and Hugo; our reader, for some obscure reason, found himself endowing Hugo Grainger with the physical attributes of Hendrik Andersen.

After all, Toby had described Hugo as tall, with bright yellow hair. Hendrik, the beloved Hendrik, was of 'magnificent stature' with Scandinavian fair locks and brilliant blue eyes. His image rose perpetually before the inner vision of our poor friend—most sorrowfully so; and, in the affection-starved life of Toby Lamb, Hugo seemed to have played a very similar role. When Hugo departed for Cambridge, what daily anguish Toby must have felt! 'I missed him with every breath,' he wrote, and our friend could only, and most profoundly, sympathise with this misery of loss.

The tragic, needless death of Moses created yet another link, recalling, as it must, the sad untimely end of Wilky James, the dear younger brother, who, never having fully regained his health after wounds received in the Civil War, had died sixteen years ago at the age of thirty-eight.

Was it for reasons such as these that the house had called out to our friend so loudly?

Then, there was the ghost; but our hero was not, in fact, precisely certain as to his own standpoint in the matter of ghosts.—He had written, it was true, various ghostly tales. What he sought in these, what he had enjoyed in youthful perusal of Poe, Hawthorne, Dickens, Wilkie Collins, Merimée, Sheridan Le Fanu, Hoffmann, Balzac, was not the conventional figure of a spectre, clanking chains and wailing, but simply the presentation of ghostly terror, haunted people—'without the stale effect of the mere bloated bugaboo'; and that was what he himself hoped to achieve in his next ghostly tale *The Sense of the Past*. He had, to be sure, visited many haunted mansions, stayed at châteaux and palazzi around which supernatural legends had been woven, had slept in significant turret rooms (the frequent quarters of bachelor guests); indeed, Lamb House itself was locally reputed to possess a ghost. Our hero's father, fifty-five years before, had undergone a supernatural experience in a cottage near Windsor, while Henry was only a baby—had become aware of an invisible shape 'squatting in the room, raying out from his fetid personality influences fatal to life'. The shock had left Henry James Senior ill and shattered for months. Elder brother William also, when a medical

'Since you ask, I will tell you.' The elder brother was clear about it. 'In the first place—has it not occurred to you—there may be, there very probably are, members of the Lamb family still in existence, for whom such a publication would be unmitigated shame and bale. Why should they suffer a degrading incident in the family past to be thus unearthed and exposed to light? In fact one might argue that they, by inheritance "own" the affair—it is not yours to publish.'

'After nearly two centuries?'

'My dear fellow—you have dealt with this kind of moral dilemma yourself, as I recall, in several of your own little stories. The idea of responsibility—whether to make public or destroy documents connected, to its great detriment, with a hitherto honoured name—I seem to remember the term *publishing scoundrel* . . . ?'

'Well;' our friend gave it some thought. 'That—*The Aspern Papers*—that affair lay at least within the bounds of living memory. Survivors of the actual events still remained. This is further into the past—'

'And,' the elder brother pursued, 'another point, which does not yet appear to have struck you: *was Toby telling the truth?*'

Our friend stared again. 'Why should he, for heaven's sake, not be?'

'For a variety of reasons. As it emerges from his narrative, Toby appears a very decent, feeling character. So he represents himself. But is that a true portrait? The facts might well be otherwise. Perhaps Toby pushed his sister Alice into the well, consumed with anger and jealousy because she had come, fatally and finally, between himself and his friend. After all, Toby had told Hugo about her past; that was not a very brotherly act.'

'Oh—brotherly! But our poor Toby was in the moral dilemma there.'

student, suffered, without any warning 'a horrible fear of my own existence'. As in his father's experience, the horror took the form of a mental patient he had once observed, a black-haired youth with a greenish skin who sat all day like a Peruvian mummy. '*That shape am I*, I felt, potentially.' William, as a result, became afraid of the dark, afraid of being left alone; without the help of religion he would 'have grown really insane'.—Alice James contained within her equal abysses; the inside of her head felt like a dense jungle, she often had a terror of falling asleep—more so towards her death, when she could only be relieved by hypnosis; she had a feeling of 'bottled lightning' inside her. The James family were, in fine, highly strung, acutely susceptible to outside influence, and subject to nervous ailments: William, Henry, and Alice all suffered from back pains, constipation, eye trouble, insomnia, dyspepsia, lack of appetite; and Alice, furthermore, suffered from menstrual pains, fainting spells, tooth decay, vomiting, hysterical fits of laughter and tears, lack of concentration.

But, an actual ghost?

Our friend himself would later on endure an extraordinary, a terrifying dream—a dream so vivid, so intolerable, that the memory of it would remain with him for the rest of his life, and become the raw material for at least two stories, embodying its hair-raising details: it began with the need to defend a portal against some awful agent, some creature of darkness which threatened him from the unthinkable regions outside the door, threatening his 'place of rest'. (Peter Quint, perhaps, outside the window?) But the dream would end in a startling reversal—the dreamer turned the tables, forced the door *outward*, chased the evil visitant away along an enormous gallery, the *galérie d'Apollon* of the Louvre, while, overhead, volleys of thunder roared and lightning flashed. In the real-life nightmare, the dreamer finally triumphed against his adversary; but in one fictionalised version, *The Jolly Corner*, the hero confronts the spectre and finds it to be the ultimate in horror—himself as he might have become had he, instead of leaving America and living a life of letters, pursued an acquisitive, money-grubbing career in the world of commerce. He is an evil, odious, blatant stranger—*vulgar—aggressive*—with two fingers on one hand reduced to stumps. Paralysed with dread, the dreamer faints away, on the black and white marble squares of childhood's dearly remembered hallway.

In another such dream (once related to Lady Ottoline Morrell) our hero enters a great mansion filled with treasures, wanders through its chambers, past their cabinets and masterpieces—but uneasy all the time, subject to a strange, ghastly malaise; then, on the upper storey, discovers an old man sitting on a chair, and shouts at him, '*You're afraid of me, you coward! . . .* I know it! I see the sweat on your brow!'

Whose fear is the greater—the haunter, or the haunted? And, indeed, who *was* the haunter, who *was* the haunted? Was the old man in the chair his father? Or his high-handed elder brother? Had it taken him all his life to come to terms with the pair of them? Or was the stranger more truly himself, his might-have-been, perhaps regretted, commercially capable self?

No wonder he felt a curious sense of admiration, of fraternal fondness, of respectful comradeship for young Toby Lamb who had, during his father's ill health, taken over the management of the brewery, who had survived the deaths of his brothers, who had succeeded his father as Mayor of Rye!—Would our friend too, perhaps, have liked to be offered the Mayoralty? Mayors of Rye had, for the past hundred years, often resided in Lamb House; he had his own pew established (though never occupied) in the

church; the notion must, sometimes, if only frivolously, have crossed his mind. It would not, though, have been feasible so long as he retained his American nationality (which, of course, he did, in the end relinquish).

Meanwhile he nourished a most eager wish to show the journal of Toby Lamb to his brother William, at present in Malvern taking the hydropathic cure, but soon to return to Rye for a Christmas visit with his wife and daughter Peggy. Our hero wanted advice, confirmation of his own intentions really, on a point of ethical procedure. Also, of course, he felt a small glow of pride. Toby was, after all, in a manner of speaking, his very own *trouvaille*, his own private forbear and ghost . . .

'You see, my dear fellow, what I am, so to speak, driving at?'

The two brothers reciprocally stared. William then thoughtfully propounded, 'It is to be a justification for your purchase of the house? Is that it? You still seek, as it were, affirmation of my approval?'

'Hang it, no! I make my own decisions. But why, now, I want you, as it were, *here* for me, is to decide on the measure of responsibility.'

'The individual himself is the only rightful chooser of his risk.'

'Oh—risk! No risk attaches to me personally; the crux, you see, is Toby. To publish his poor little story would be, in my—'

'Publish?' William took a moment over that. 'You would really carry out such a step?'

The tone of dubiety and scepticism was enough to our friend.

'It belongs to a series of possibilities. The whole thing lies so before one. And why in the world, after all, should not I?'

William went on. 'One way to reach a conclusion in this questionable matter would be to unearth the true story. Have you, in point of fact, made any effort to discover whether the occurrences in Toby's narrative do have any firm basis in historical fact? Have you "read up" the Lamb family?'

'On the contrary.' Our friend frowned. 'You know my dislike of being furnished with superfluous detail. People *will* talk so and tiresomely over-elaborate when they offer one a "nugget" and fill in just those areas which one would most immensely prefer kept in a state of fertile emptiness and mystery—'

Now it was the elder brother's turn for surprise.

'You mean that you *yourself* propose to make use—?'

'But of course. You cannot, surely, have imagined otherwise?'

William had a momentary silence.

'*Not*, you mean, publish Toby's journal as it stands?'

'Toby is, as he stands, irreflectively juvenile; his work is not "written" at all, poor dear fellow; because of his—so mistakenly—adhering to a first-person narrative, he has allowed himself no means of passing, at the critical moment, from the consciousness of one character to that of another. It would be doing him no justice to allow the poor boy to appear before the public in the person that he has, so to speak, presented himself as being. It would indeed be doing him the greatest disservice in the world; I have grave doubts as to whether any editor would, as it were, even invite him over the threshold.'

William took another pause.

'Your plan, then, would be to "rewrite" Toby?'

'But of course. How could I not? Was it not, in fine, for that sole purpose that the poor dear little house in its own way so exigently summoned me? It wanted, it demanded, a particular kind of inmate.'

'Of which you are the example?'

'Of which I am the example.'

'But what then, as you see it, is your part?'

'My part takes the form of wanting to be sovereignly and sublimely *helpful* to young Toby. To teach him. That is, in vulgar phrase, a large order, but I'm not afraid of it!'

William's response had an abruptness. 'But have you the right?'

'My dear brother—why, do you think, otherwise, should the house have, in its own fashion "chosen" me? I now understand, in fact, that its influence was felt by me— unconsciously—long before the appearance of Toby's journal. What else prompted me to write *The Turn of the Screw*—a tale of two abused, unfortunate children in a country mansion? I had been, I apprehend, "approaching" Toby for many months before the ultimate discovery. And now his burden lies on me.'

'How, by the bye, do you "see" Toby?' William spoke not idly, but with a keen and piercing look.

Our friend took time to consider.

'How do I see Toby? Young Toby? I see him as always placing a low value on himself—as wishing for ever to be some other, happier, more fortunate person. As being governed by random circumstances during his childhood, and by other people's irresponsibilities. As being, often, rather sick and sorry. I see him as a young creature, shy, vulnerable, lacking confidence, but not bad looking; and, despite all, filled with hope.'

'As yourself at that age, in fact? You plant yourself solidly in Toby's shoes! And there lies the danger! Now, my dear boy, here is how I see the matter: if you feel so sure that Toby's mysterious debt to the universe could not, will not, be adequately paid off by our simple perusal of his journal, there could be, for instance, a recourse to mediumistic assistance.'

Our author had a wince of distaste.

'The dreadful Mrs Piper? Such so-called "mediums" do more to degrade spiritual conception than the grossest forms of materialism. I would certainly not dream of submitting our poor young Toby to such usage.'

Paying no heed to this, William pursued: 'It seems to me quite credible that Toby Lamb—or some such entity—may still frequent this location and, as it were, focus itself, to the best of its ability, on some living consciousness.'

Our friend considered, 'Perhaps. If you say so! But what if, by now—it is, after all, nearly two hundred years— young Toby has, in some way, changed his views?'

'Changed?'

'I recall you once said that some infernality of the body might prevent, during life, parts of the mind coming to their effective rights. That when the essence of mind passes out of the body, there may be an explosion of liberated force. If such an outcome had been the case for Toby, he might—by now—have the very strongest objections to being, as you put it, summoned by Mrs Piper.'

William threw this off. 'If so, my dear boy, you demolish your own argument. Where is your premise for believing that the house—or Toby's "dynamic" in it—wishes to have his story made known?'

Our friend hung fire for a moment, then emphatically returned, 'Why, otherwise, create the chain of circumstances leading to the conflagration in the Green Room? The discovery of Toby's journal? Why offer it to *me*—of all possible recipients?'

'Because—it may be—of your expert knowledge in publishing matters. Your "connections".'

'In that case,' protested our writer with a certain sharpness, 'in that case almost any practitioner in the writing trade would suffice. Why make so particular a point of, as it were, stipulating that the services called for should be mine?'

William considered. 'Very likely because of the parallels—which you yourself have remarked upon. The sister, the brother. The disability. These factors, it may be, have rendered you especially susceptible to the place's message.'

'It is true,' the younger brother observed, meditating on this, 'that I should dearly like to write a story about the peculiar, intense and interesting affection between a brother and a sister. For a writer such as myself, Toby's little narrative would be no more than the springboard; no possible connections could be drawn between his tiny radius and the surpassing curve of the finished creation.'

William frowned. 'You mean—you would work it up, by dint of descriptions and psychologising, and so forth, into something five times as long—in the way you did with *The Bostonians*, which, at, say, a hundred pages, could have been a light, bright, sparkling thing?'

'I should make my own particular use of it,' the younger brother somewhat stiffly returned.

'My dear boy: I very much doubt if you have the right to do that. How can you be sure that would satisfy Toby's wish? As I see it, he wants *his* journal published. We are both agreed—for differing reasons, mine moral, yours—ah—professional—that that would not be suitable. But I do *not* believe that you have been granted carte blanche to tamper with the story. No; all things considered, I think young Toby must, for the time being, possess his poor soul in patience; the moment has not yet come for his story—or Alice's story—to meet the light of day.'

Our hero had a profound drop. 'You mean—do *nothing*?'

'Do precisely nothing. Restore the journal to the cupboard—brick it up again. Leave it, with sympathy, alone.

Toby's wish must not necessarily be your guide in this.'

The tea-bell sounded, perhaps fortunately, at this juncture, and William's wife called from downstairs, 'Come along, you idle pair of men! You have been talking up there the whole afternoon, while Peggy and I braved the snowstorm and have walked three times round Church Square. The marsh is all veiled in mist, and Rye is like a besieged town!'

'Yes,' agreed her daughter, 'and the wind is rising to a regular New England blizzard. It will be a grand night for ghost stories, so I hope that you have one to read us, Uncle Henry!'

'Well, I do have one, my dear Peggott, since you ask,' her uncle told her, taking his seat, 'and located, by the bye, in this very house.'

Catching a very keen glance from his brother, he explained, smiling, 'It is an *invented* ghostly tale, William, about two maiden ladies and a raffish, phantom ancestor.'

'Perfect, Uncle Henry. Delicious! As a reward, here is your tea.'

'Did it ever occur to you, Henry,' inquired his sister-in-law, handing her host a dish of toasted tea-cakes, 'did it ever occur to you that the ghost seen in the garden by the Lamb family—yes, thanks to your kind permission I, too, have been slowly poring my way through Toby's journal—did you ever stop to consider that their ghost bears a remarkably strong resemblance to yourself? A man in black, wearing a square black hat—how often have I not seen you retire to your Garden Room wearing that square black Holbein smoking cap of yours? And the black velvet jacket? Ghosts, I suppose, may be the images sent us from the future, just as readily as from the past?'

Her brother-in-law stared, greatly taken aback at this novel conception. 'My dear, I never even considered such a possibility.'

'But, seriously, Henry, have you—yourself—ever seen anything in the slightest degree supernatural, or at all out of the ordinary, in this delightful, snug, welcoming little residence of yours?'

He considered. 'Seen' anything, no, that he had not. But guessed at, doubted, sensed, received multifarious 'impressions', not through any of his five senses, but through some transcendental metaphysical medium, that he certainly had.

And the sum total of all these infinitely faint, infinitely subtle 'hints' falling on his mind like flakes of soot from a fire, amounted to a picture—a picture of a boy, a boy whose presence had never quite left the house and garden, a boy lame but active, forlorn but hopeful, neglected but with great capacity for love.

These things remained unspoken and unspeakable. 'My dear Alice—in a word—no,' he at last rejoined, and at the very same instant felt the house settle itself a little, shrug, as it were, its shoulders, shift itself in a kind of premonitory quiver—recalling the earthquake in Florence—before, in silence, disposing itself to hear him read aloud his charming and light-hearted story entitled *The Third Person*.

After the tale had been applauded: 'What would you think, Henry,' inquired his brother, 'of my trying an experiment in mesmerism on you? It is possible, as you suggested earlier, that you are more "in touch" with the Lamb family than you may, in full consciousness, apprehend.—And don't forget, I beg you, what a beneficent effect hypnosis had on our poor sister during her last weeks.'

Our writer gave a shudder. 'My dear and respected brother, no! As a therapeutic measure for poor Alice I don't deny its efficacy, but to have it used upon my helpless self as a kind of spiritual *pick-lock*—a thousand times, no! I have no intention of being ever, voluntarily, in anything but full conscious control of such faculties as I possess—'

'Pray do not tempt Providence, my dear fellow!' begged his brother. '—And do bear in mind what I have said about not subjecting members of the Lamb family to needless distress and publicity by launching Toby's story on to the world. Even supposing you were to, as you proposed, make your own thing of it—who knows, they might well, in view of where you are, all too readily put two and two together . . .'

The William Jameses departed southward, in mid-January, to a borrowed château in Costebelle, on the French Riviera.

Our friend had been deeply unsettled by their visit, especially by his senior's avowed disapproval, amounting almost to an interdict, of the novelist's plan to rework and publish Toby Lamb's journal. Frustrated in this intention, yet needing the routine of work, both as a tranquilliser and to provide funds for his purchase of the house, our writer therefore occupied himself in the production of a number of rather sharp and spiteful short stories. Then, still imbued with the idea of, as it were, participating in Toby's recollections, he embarked on a longer work, the title and germ of which he had already by him. It was to be called *The Sense of the Past*, and would itself be a species of ghostly tale, concerned with a young American, on a visit to the home of his English ancestors, finding himself carried back, translated mysteriously into an earlier period. Mark Twain had done something of the sort ten years earlier, but his was a satire, whereas our writer's would be of a more serious nature. The period selected was the early nineteenth century, 1820, not long before the writer's own familial boundaries. If only Toby Lamb's journal had been set then, instead of a hundred years previously! Caught in a yearning to describe the past, yet lacking the needful data, the writer's invention flagged and failed.

Regretful, dissatisfied, after a hundred and ten pages,

he set the work on one side. It was not to be resumed for another fourteen years. Instead, as spring drew on, he found himself engaged on a study of relationships; of, indeed, the James family theory that one person's achievement must always be balanced by another's failure, that in a relationship between two people there can never be equality, but the first one's health is inevitably paid for by the decline of the second, or one's increase in wit by the other's lapse into dullness. And, indeed, one life might be paid for by the other's *death*. Had Alice Lamb, perhaps, died that Toby might live?

Our friend had intended *The Sacred Fount* to be no more than a 10,000-word story. He had begun it with some vague notion, also, of 'showing young Toby' how, if that uncouth vehicle a first-person narrative should by any chance be undertaken, it must be handled. It had, unfortunately, grown out of all proportion to its content. And now he was greatly absorbed in another plot: the story of an American sent to Paris to rescue a young kinsman who had fallen into undesirable hands. At times, though, he was suffused by a sense of unfulfilled responsibility towards poor Toby. I will come back to you, Toby, I will indeed, he promised silently; you shall be vindicated; I shall contrive to do it in such a way that nobody need take offence.—And he thought he felt his fellow-inmate settle down again humbly, patiently, prepared to wait.

Meanwhile our hero wrote to Hendrik Andersen:

I feel, my dear boy, my arms around you; lacking your own dear presence—or even one of your newer and so monumental works—I have discovered, in an unobtrusive, musty emporium, close to the cattle-market, in the lower regions of little restful red-roofed uncomplicated Rye, a worn stone statue, part of some now-crumbled and dismantled piece of decorative masonry, which has, to my delight, a most striking and unambiguous resemblance to your dear handsome self. I have had it established under the mulberry tree in the midst of my ill-found rosebed, and it comforts and charms me greatly—in default of him whom it represents. But when, dear Boy, will you *yourself* return? My heart aches for you. You may have, at any time, undisputed rule over my Watchbell Lane studio—your room, your welcome, your place, everywhere, are here waiting for you!

Hendrik, however, was busy elsewhere, and did not come.

In May our writer was suddenly impelled to shave off his beard. 'It had suddenly begun, these three months since, to come out quite white and made me feel, as well as look, so old,' he wrote to William, who may have been somewhat irritated at this younger-brotherly preening, since he was himself still far from well.

Our friend now sat, clean-shaven, for a portrait painted by his cousin Bay; he met, in the course of the ensuing months, the odd random assemblage of other writers—Crane, Conrad, Ford Madox Ford, Wells—who, by chance, at that period lived around or near Rye; he wrote *The Ambassadors*, and then *The Wings of the Dove*, all the time with Toby a faintly poignant presence at the back of his mind. Soon, soon! he promised.

Then, late in 1902, our writer had a chance to see, in the vault of a local bank, an object which had belonged to the Lamb family, that very christening goblet presented by King George I to Toby's younger brother George, a large silver-gilt bowl. It had 'a grand style and capacity', he wrote to a descendant of the Lamb family (whose existence justified all William's apprehensions). The bowl provided for our hero a *point d'appui*; he was immediately imbued with a strong wish to write a story about it; at the same time, by undertaking this, he felt that he was in some fashion

145

fulfilling part of his debt to Toby. He began to write *The Golden Bowl*.

Earlier that summer the William Jameses had returned to Rye, and William had dictated some of his lectures on *Varieties of Religious Experience* to his brother's new secretary, Miss Weld; then, at the end of the summer, William and Alice had returned to America (to our hero's relief), William upholding to the last his considered opinion that the journal of Toby Lamb should neither be published nor tampered with.

The document therefore remained locked away in our friend's desk drawer, month after month, and then year after year.

After completing *The Golden Bowl*—which took him the most part of two years—our friend sailed the Atlantic to his homeland, the first such voyage for many years; he visited his brother, toured, lectured, made notes for his book *The American Scene*; then returned to England, began revising his complete works for the definitive New York edition; and became marginally involved, once again, with the English theatre.

During all this time Toby's voice remained a faint, a very faint, ghostly and remote cry. Not wholly unheeded, not forgotten, but relegated, as it were, to a side chapel, some quiet unlit corner far from the central activity of nave and altar.

The house made no move. It bided its time.

In 1909 young Hugh Walpole came to Rye, to stay at Lamb House.

He was a charming, ambitious, good-looking young writer who had had a difficult childhood: son of a bishop, brought up lovingly, during his early years, in a gentle cultivated home in New Zealand, he was then abruptly catapulted into the mayhem and jungle of an English public school. This experience, though he professed to have surmounted it, had in fact left him spiritually maimed, one of the symptoms being an insatiable need for love and approval. The love he was to receive, in abundance, from our friend, whom he met in February 1909; the approval, from the Master, over the next few years, would be much more qualified, and contain a touch of satire: 'You bleat and jump like a white lambkin on the vast epistolary green ...' However our writer was more than happy (lacking Hendrik) to invite the young man in April to Lamb House, and he was installed with due honour in the King's Chamber.

Next day the youthful guest came to breakfast looking white, shaken, and ten years older than he had the evening before.

His host was deeply, melodiously, paternally concerned.

'My dearest boy! What is amiss? You look—*lamentable*—waxen—unstrung—are you ill? What can have happened? Shall I send for the good Doctor Skinner?'

Walpole explained, however, that he was not ill; merely suffering from the after effects of a calamitous, a horrendous dream.

'It was—I can't describe it—I was back at school again; you don't, *cher maître*, thank God, know anything about the horrors, the unspeakable horrors of an English public school—'

The Master exhaled. 'No—for which I can see I may be for ever thankful to Providence and to the migratory habits of my little fat Swedenborgian amateur of a father—who, wherever he sent us, never, mercifully, left us there for long; the worst, I suppose, was that excellent establishment the *Institution Rochette*—where they tried in vain to persuade an understanding of mathematics into my skull—but I digress, my dear child—your dream—?'

'Oh, it was so awful. Well—you see—when I was a very little boy, everybody told me—I had a complete belief—that anyone who was gently reared, well behaved, who said his prayers daily and trusted in God and acted kindly to others—I understood, I knew, that such a person would receive the same usage back from the rest of the world.'

'Not unreasonably, my dearest boy. Though—I fear—a belief soon subject to revision—'

'*Revision!*' The younger man took this with scornful indulgence. 'It was just wickedly false. The case was totally otherwise. I had to take in—at the age of eleven—having spent the years up till then in the company of gentle, civilised people who loved me—suddenly I had to comprehend that the world was not like that *at all*—but was in fact composed of violence, brutality, squalor, degradation, and filth. That was a lesson never to be unlearned. And my dream last night sent me back to that time.'

'Spare me the details, my dear boy, I beg,' his host besought him with uplifted hands.

'Oh, I shall. They are too—Well, the *simplest*, the *mildest* thing they did to new boys at Crale—at my school—was to hang you up in front of a hot fire and roast you, until you fainted. That was at least clean, decent pain. But—'

'Please!'

'No, but the worst part of my dream, I was going to tell you, was that the victim—strangely enough—was not myself, but a boy called Alice—'

'*A boy called Alice?*'

'They mocked him, they told him he was really a girl. He was a gentle, plump, dark-eyed lad—trustful and unafraid when he arrived—oh, the things they did to him—it was the Pit, the ultimate horror—'

'Try not to think about it, my darling boy. Let us only be thankful that it was only a dream; that it is over.'

The host himself looked almost as white and shaken as his guest; several times he passed an unsteady hand over his large brow. 'We will move you, tonight, to a different chamber, dear fellow; perhaps that room, that bed, that situation, did not agree with you. Come: let us go out into the cheerful air; my garden, with its primulas and daffodils, shall comfort you—'

Leaving their meal (porridge with cream, and three scrambled eggs apiece) for the most part uneaten, the two men passed out into the sunshine. With due pride, the host showed off the garden's April glories, and then led his young friend to inspect the newly acquired statue, set up under the mulberry tree, which he had bought because it had a look of Hendrik, his other so neglectful and evasive darling.

'Does it *recall* anybody to you?' he asked wistfully—though aware that Hugh and Hendrik had probably never met, for the latter had his studio in Rome. But Hugh responded, in a puzzled and tremulous tone, 'Why, yes, sir—it does—it seems to bear the strangest resemblance to the boy called Alice in my dream . . .'

Despite this unfortunate start, the weekend visit was a happy one. Hugh wrote in his diary: 'The house and garden are exactly suited to him. He is beyond words. I cannot speak about him.'

Our friend did not, though strongly tempted, show Toby's journal to Hugh. He spoke of it, he described it. And then, on a later visit, it was at last brought out, the host first taking the precaution of asking that his young friend should not mention the manuscript to anybody.

'Do you notice a change in that statue out there in the rose bed?' our hero asked his servant, the faithful Burgess in the autumn of 1909. The latter, after scratching his head, replied, 'Why, yes, sir, now you come to mention it, the thing *do* seem to have weathered up most uncommon, more'n you'd think it would do, in the time since Gammon and me set it out there.'

'Singular! Most singular!'

Even to his own puzzled, anxious eye, the figure no longer seemed to resemble dear Hendrik. And, over the following months, it continued to change, to shrink, to crumble.

During this period our friend became deeply depressed, and, several times, felt obliged to consult Dr Skinner over a fancied indisposition of the heart. Skinner, at last, sent him to London to consult a specialist. The latter, Sir James Mackenzie, was encouraging. He could find no cause for alarm. But his patient did not wholly believe in these reassurances. Through autumn and winter he became more and more troubled and despondent. It was like the old days, when William's presence in the house had operated on him like heavy atmospheric pressure, burdening his health, spirits, mental activity, with a weight under which they could not function. His image of the boy Toby had begun to change: he no longer envisaged his incorporeal companion as a young, ingenuous, confiding creature, peacefully, patiently engaged about his daily duties in house and garden; but rather he was to be apprehended as a haggard, troubled being, not now in first youth, but with hair beginning to recede and a sad recurrence of his former limp, always, too, with a look of strained, painful expectation on his pale countenance, as if he waited perpetually for the sound of carriage wheels, or of hoofbeats that never came.

And, at night, our writer had regular dreams of a woman who seemed unceasingly angry.

'You never give yourself entirely—do you?' she threw at him. 'Always, always, something is kept in reserve for your work. *Your work!* That is your privilege. Whereas *my* existence must be patched together between duties to others. That was all I ever had. My greatest sin was to send the maid out for a chocolate cake. Imagine it—in my wretched, trammelled life I was not even allowed the luxury of swearing. The word *damn* was forbidden territory.'

'Don't scold, dear Alice!' he begged. 'I did not make those rules.'

'*I am not your dear Alice!*'

In a mood of propitiation, hopeless grief, impatience, despair, our poor writer removed from his study at Lamb House an enormous pile of private papers, carried them into the wintry garden, and immolated them on the gardener's bonfire: letters, manuscripts, notebooks, sketches for as yet unwritten works—all, all went up in smoke, the literary treasures of half a century.

There, Toby! he cried internally. You observe, I value my own residue as being of less worth than your little story. Yours I keep; mine, I destroy. A sacrifice to your understanding . . .

For a short while after that, the Master felt himself better, felt able to plan a new piece of work. 'My poor old blest Genius pats me so admirably and lovingly on the back that I turn, I screw round, and bend my lips to passionately, in my gratitude, kiss its hand . . . Causons, causons, mon bon . . .'

But the respite was transitory. Burning the papers did not, for long, appease his Furies or assist his mental state. Never at any time a heavy sleeper, he now found it almost impossible to sleep at all. A ration of an hour a night was the maximum. But what to do in all this hateful time, with no work to occupy his mind? Idle thoughts rattled like castanets. Food became loathsome to him. The doctor, growing anxious, prescribed bed-rest and a nurse. His brother William, deeply concerned (he had had a 'very pathetic' letter from Henry) despatched his son Harry across the Atlantic to find out how the invalid really did.

Harry's report was not reassuring. 'There was nothing for me to do but to sit by his side and hold his hand while he panted and sobbed for two hours until the Doctor arrived . . . He talked about Aunt Alice and his own end . . . the next day the same thing began again with a fear of being alone. Sometimes he called me Toby . . .'

And the Master's kind friend Edith Wharton wrote: 'I could hardly believe it was the same James who cried out to me his fear, his despair, his craving for "the cessation of consciousness", & all his unspeakable loneliness & need of comfort, & inability to be comforted!'

William and his wife decided that they had better come to England; William, on the written evidence, was able to diagnose that his brother was suffering from melancholia, or nervous breakdown. The writer himself termed it 'the black devils of nervousness, direct damnedest demons.' 'I have really been down into hell,' he was later to say. William, whose heart condition was once again very serious, would travel on to Bad Nauheim for another cure, while his wife Alice remained in Lamb House to cheer and comfort her afflicted brother-in-law. (She even attempted to teach him to knit, but without success.) Poor lady! she would much rather have been ministering to her own husband.

In June the pair crossed to Germany to join William who, alas, had not been helped by the cure. In August the three set sail for Quebec, both brothers in desperately low health and spirits. Their remaining brother, Robertson, had died not long before.

And, at the end of August, William, now back at home in Chocorua, also died.

'Ideal Elder Brother,' wrote his junior. *'I was always his absolute younger and smaller.'*

Our friend passed the winter in Cambridge, Massachusetts, endeavouring to console his widowed sister-in-law, who exasperated him by holding seances in an effort to summon William's spirit. But, perhaps fortunately, the spirit made no response to these calls.

At last feeling a little better, he began to write again, grew homesick for England, and sailed back in July 1911. Returned to Lamb House, he found that he still felt unhappily *caged* there—in some indefinable manner threatened—so left again for London, where he embarked on a memorial to his father and brother.

Removing himself to London he also, at the same time, withdrew Toby Lamb's journal from its resting-place in the desk drawer, and placed it among his luggage.

Sad, dreadfully, and permanently depriving as was the fact of his brother's death, yet it had liberated him from one of the blocks that had consigned him to such a low ebb of misery. In the matter of Toby's journal he now felt that it might, soon, be possible to take some action. Causons, causons, mon bon . . .

The following year, still feeling a strange dread of, and disinclination for, Lamb House, our writer lent it to his nephew Billy and new wife Alice for a honeymoon period. Let the haggard presence of Toby lean over their shoulders if he must.—So yet another Alice, a third (who knows, perhaps a fourth?) walked the garden paths and climbed the wide shallow stairs of Lamb House.

In the spring of 1912 our friend returned, at long last, to Rye, bearing with him Toby Lamb's manuscript, still unpublished, and, as well, a new, most meticulously written version of Toby's story.

He had called it *The Shade in the Alley*, and, he flattered himself, it could give no possible distress to any surviving members of the family, for he had taken the greatest pains to obliterate any possible direct references or connections.

With rare and uncharacteristic diffidence he did not immediately despatch the text of his own story to the agent J.B. Pinker who now acted for him, but, instead, waited for a visit from Edith Wharton—whom he sometimes termed an angel, sometimes an eagle, and, more recently, 'the Firebird' or 'the dear of dears'.

Their first encounter had been more than twenty years ago, in Paris, but that meeting was so trivial that our friend had no recollection of the occasion. In 1899 she had humbly presented him with a copy of her first book of tales, *The Greater Inclination*, but it had taken him over a year to thank her for it. He recognised the (partly unconscious) flattery in the fact that she had modelled her style on his, and, when he did acknowledge the gift, wrote kindly, praising her 'admirable sharpness and neatness', adding, as was his wont, various critical remarks, but also inviting her to show him her future work.

From then on their friendship had burgeoned. She, a New Yorker by birth, wealthy, conducting a pendulum existence between America and cosmopolite expatriatism in Europe, would, from time to time, invite our friend for visits to her Parisian establishment in the rue de Varenne, where, he reported, he suffered from 'an indigestion of chère Madame', but nonetheless hugely enjoyed the experience; or, accompanied by her husband Teddy, she would dart about England in her chauffeur-driven Panhard, descending upon our bedazzled author and carrying him away for exhilarating trips across the country and to various great houses, despite his protests at the waste of writing-time. She herself, meanwhile, continued to produce novels and these, beginning with *The House of Mirth* in 1905, received considerable acclaim and sold, as her poor august friend never failed to point out, very much better than his own. His tone of playfulness on these occasions did not entirely mask the puzzled hurt which accompanied the knowledge. His own works were great, were monumental; he could not but be aware of their stature; why, then, did they sell so badly, why was his public so limited, compared with hers?

It was in a mood of unusual humility, therefore, that, when the 'bird o' Freedom' next arrived in Rye, on the 20th of July, he put to her his cautious request. Would she, could she read *The Shade in the Alley* and give him her honest opinion of it. Much gratified, naturally, she promised to do so, but the moment just then was not propitious; she asked permission to carry it with her on the round of visits they now proposed paying, and was accordingly supplied with a carbon copy.—He did not show her Toby's original.

During the series of visits—which included days spent at Hill Hall, with Howard Sturgis at Queen's Acre, at Cliveden (Lady Astor) and Newbury (Lady St Halier, who proved, however, to be away from home) no time could be found to read the story; our friend, not surprisingly, suffered from two minor heart attacks, and, after a second visit to Howard Sturgis, the writer was returned, solicitously, by car and chauffeur, on the 2nd of August, to his own house.

'Went straight to bed,' he wrote.

However on the 12th of August Mrs Wharton returned to Rye, en route for the Continent.

After lunch, Teddy having been despatched for a ramble round Rye, our author at last seized the bull by the horns and requested his guest's opinion of the story.

'Being only too well aware of your own prowess as a proficient of what might be termed ghostly tales, I have the utmost confidence in soliciting the expert comment of an associate, a fellow-artist; not only that but a, to put it in its simplest terms, member of the opposite sex. Did it, so to speak, achieve its object? Did it, ah, thwack the, as it were, nail, on the head?'

Mrs Wharton's charming round brown face disposed itself into thoughtful creases; her bright hazel eyes clouded. She took a pause.

The lunch served that day at Lamb House had not, to her mind, been a good one. In the past she (a lavish hostess, famous for hospitality) had had occasion to comment several times, in the privacy of her diary, upon the 'anxious frugality' shown in the Master's establishment, on the 'dreary pudding or pie of which a quarter or a half had been consumed at dinner' reappearing on the table next day for lunch with its ravages unimpaired. The meal served that day, in her estimation, was hardly above the nursery shepherds'-pie-and-rice-pudding level—tasty enough of its kind, doubtless, but hardly what she, after many former instances of her own liberality to her host, felt was owing to her. True, the claret had been excellent, but still—! She resolved to be candid.

'My dear—I was coming to it, I had not forgotten,' she said. 'That was why I sent Teddy out to Ypres Castle. Your story is too sublime, too wonderful, of course—it is surpassingly, magnificently *you*—But, I ask myself, I have spent these last ten days in perplexity wondering—is it Tod?'

Dismayed, concerned, confounded, not so much by her tone as by the look in her fine eyes, he requested amplification.

'Cher Maître'—she had a smile for him, as if to mitigate the stringencies of what she had to say, 'where was your motive in, as you did, suspending your central characters so completely in a void? Tod—Huon—Agnes—you miraculously work on them, you breathe on them and around them with consummate art, you play on them strange beams of diffused, refracted light, you sound, all about them, wandering airs of Aeolian harp music—and yet you have stripped them of the human fringes we necessarily trail after us through life. Your characters are tremendous, they are exquisite, but we never, so to speak, see them *au naturel*, brushing their hair, or eating a slice of bread-and-butter.—And yet your Tod, you give us to understand, was a hopeful, kindly, imaginative boy, Agnes was a sweet simple friendly girl—until the Furies caught up with her; but all the poor reader sees of them is a kind of golden, swirling dusty mist. Very rare, to be sure, very ravishing, but, as a diet, not adequate nourishment. Indeed, rather suffocating! And then, your setting, this dear, comfortable, snug little house, this cosy, enchanting little town (for I guess I am not wrong in divining that is where the story is laid) where are *they*? Vanished, dissolved, melted away off the edge of the map! You have done them no justice, you have turned your back on them.—I believe, my dearest Master, that, in a ghost story—particularly in a ghost story—what the reader requires is *details*—the pattern on a chair, the lustre on a dish—in order to form a striking contrast against the unearthly secrets that you, the writer, are going to impart or, if nothing else, hint at. But you, dear Master, maintain the whole thing, as it were, in mid-air; you never allow your reader a glimpse of the kind of life your characters are supposed to lead when they are, so to speak, off-stage. Tell me now, why—most particularly in this story—did you do that?'

Our writer, turning enormous perturbed grey eyes on his visitor, answered in a shaken voice, 'My dear—I didn't know I had!'

'Now, in *The Turn of the Screw*,' she remorselessly pursued, '—which is a masterpiece, a heart-chilling work of superb art, and one that will remain for ever in the memory of any person who reads it—there, cher Maître, you managed quite otherwise. And it needs no humble acolyte such as myself to point out to you wherein the difference lies—but I will point it out nevertheless. It is because, in that story, you permit yourself the indulgence of a first-person narrator. So, your feet—or, rather, your little governess's feet—are firmly and permanently on the ground of Bly, her eyes are fixed on the turrets of the house, or staring across the lake, we know that the old trees make a pleasant shade, and that she is engaged on a piece of stitchwork, because she *says* so—and, by limiting yourself to her single vision, her single utterance, you, if I may say so, dear Master, also keep your*self* within the grateful compass of your poor earthbound, limited reader—such as myself—who finds it sometimes such a formidable, such a Herculean task to follow you in your higher and more complicated flights! We *can* follow here, dimly, the clue that Agnes is the main character, but what her wishes are, her fears, hopes, sufferings, we never sufficiently grasp; young Tod is even more indistinct; and as for Huon, he never comes to life at all. Nothing comes through, save that he is surpassingly handsome! Dear Master, you asked me for my candid opinion; now I have given it to you.'

Our friend paused for a number of minutes before taking her up.

'Then what—' he spoke at last, in a tone somewhat deeper and hoarser than his normal one—'what, then, my dear, in the light of all this that you have just explained to me in your so delightfully sympathetic and "right" yet so piercingly explicit, and to the purpose, manner—what would you,' he rather shakily repeated, 'what would you, in fine, think it best to *do* with the little work?'

'Why, it's of a simplicity! No words that you have ever written can be wasted, dear Master. My advice is this: allow young Tod to tell his *own* story—quite straightforwardly and naturally—as he might, in his own words, had he been a real eighteenth-century boy, have done so. And preserve all these beauties—' she tapped the manuscript—'all these surpassing arabesques of invention for some other, some future tale of a more complicated form.'

He looked at her, stricken. 'Ah, my good friend—'

For a moment his hand hovered, hesitating, near the handle of the desk drawer.

But voices downstairs proclaimed the return of Teddy Wharton, who was calling, 'Edith, my dear girl, we must leave, we must be on our way, Cook tells me there is no time to be lost if we are to catch the Folkestone packet.'

In ten minutes the Whartons *were* on their way, with no more said as to *The Shade in the Alley*, or Toby Lamb.

But, as host and guests assembled outside the house in West Street, while the Whartons prepared to enter their limousine, with all the paraphernalia of goggles, motoring veils, rugs, parasols, gloves, dusters, and eau-de-Cologne, Teddy Wharton, turning kindly to survey Lamb House's friendly red-brick facade, remarked,

'Aye, it's a neat little house for a writer, Henry. I guess, after you die, they'll convert the old place into a museum—hey? Kind of shrine, would you think? Yes, *sir*!—that's, likely, what they'll do! Maybe fix it up into that top-notch English writer's residence—you know the one I mean—the poet-fellow whose job it is to turn out an ode for the king's birthday, what the devil's his name—Alfred Austin—'

'The Poet Laureate, you mean, Teddy,' his wife indulgently told him. 'But I doubt if *he* would wish to leave his present accommodation. It is a charming notion for the next century though—a literary shrine, here in Rye, perhaps dedicated to the use of young writers who might occupy the house at a peppercorn rent—is not that the English term, dear Master?'

Their host, however, austerely remarked that his intention was to bequeath the house to one of his nephews 'who can, of course, once I am gone, do with it entirely as he pleases. Goodbye, my *dear*, my *dearest* friends—a safe and a pleasant journey to you.'

And he watched them drive away down West Street with decidedly mixed feelings.

Re-entering his house, our writer entertained, for the first time, the queer sensation that it did not entirely trust him. The house, he fancifully thought, had heard that suggestion of Teddy Wharton—dear, thick-skinned, simple fellow!—had, as it were, 'taken in' the proposal and was now, in a wholly new silence, affronting its destiny. And that with no immediate welcome. Instead of a lively mix of generations, the discords, joys, and pulsations of human family life, the poor building was doomed to be a receptacle only for continual silent intense inturned literary endeavour. Was that to be its fate? Our friend received the impression, half disturbing, half mocking, that his house accommodated itself to this prospect only with the very greatest reservation, if not with downright distaste.

Sighing, our friend put away both manuscripts in a box—Toby's journal and *The Shade in the Alley*. Some hour, some voice in the future, would reveal to him the proper course . . .

1913 was in many ways a notable year for our friend. He celebrated his seventieth birthday, and his many well-wishers and friends, some three hundred of them, marked the occasion by giving him a golden bowl, a bust of himself, and his own portrait painted by Sargent.

Summer—the last summer he was to spend at Lamb House—brought with it a smaller than usual procession of visitors; and his activities were somewhat restricted because of a fainting spell in the spring. 'The evening of life is difficult,' he wrote. He found himself able, however, to complete his memoir *Notes of a Son and Brother*. He felt Toby a melancholy, resigned, slightly grim presence about the house.

A visit from the beloved young Hugh Walpole, in early autumn, began less happily than usual. Hugh was at last shown Toby's journal, which he read with mild interest, but he complained that his host's mind seemed curiously removed, most of the time, as if they talked to one another through a screen of glass.

What Hugh meant, in point of fact, was that he himself was not receiving enough attention.

'Are you ill, dear Master? You seem so restless—nervously abrupt—I feel almost that you have renounced me, that I have dropped out of your life. You spend a great deal of time—more, perhaps, than is wise?—in the contemplation of that statue out there under the mulberry tree; and, for the last two evenings, we have talked of nothing but the journal of Toby Lamb. Why, you seem, at present, to live only for and in the memory of this dead-and-gone Toby. But is that sane, dear Master? Is it sensible?'

His voice was more than a little injured at the thought of his own displacement by a being who had not been seen above ground for more than a hundred years.

'Hang that wretched Toby Lamb!' he ingenuously exclaimed. 'How about me? How about my *Mr Perrin and Mr Traill*? Have you read it yet?'

'Of course I have read it. And, naturally, took an immense interest in what you were attempting. But, my dearest boy, your Mr Traill appears to me to come through as a character with no capacity for experience—in a word, as a figment—'

During the slow unrolling of the long and devastatingly thorough criticism that followed, Hugh began to wish that he had left well alone.

'Never mind—never mind!' he begged. And, to distract

his elderly friend, he, half-jocularly inquired, 'Have you ever, in truth, actually *seen* the ghost of Toby Lamb? Or Alice Lamb?'

'Why—since you ask me—and, in point of fact—ah—that is to say—'

Disentangling, as best he could, the Master's parentheses, Hugh came to the conclusion that something had been seen, or had been felt; but, as to precisely what that something had been, he felt fairly certain that no definite information would ever be forthcoming. His host, however, disconcerted him by suddenly fixing him with a preternaturally acute and penetrative grey glare, then demanding,

'Why do you ask, my beloved boy? Is it possible that you yourself have had the impression that you were in the vicinity of some manifestation?—You have never again, I do most sincerely hope, fallen prey to that indescribably dreadful dream?'

No, Hugh said, he had not, but he had sometimes, he confessed, when alone in a corner of the house or garden, particularly the garden, been subject to the impression that he was in the company of *children*—that they were not far from him, wistfully latent, just out of sight, waiting, hoping for some eventuality, but he had no idea what—

'How many children?' his host put it to him in a tone of some eagerness.

'Well, there you have me. More than one, certainly; for I feel they confer together.'

'Ah—boys or girls?'

Both, Hugh thought. 'Some of each.'

'Interesting. Very interesting.—Perhaps the house has a different variety of manifestation for each individual witness.' The Master sighed, and took a turn about the room—they were sitting by the first fire of autumn, and a log, splitting softly, crumbled and sank down into its glowing heart.

'Would you object to witnessing a small ceremony, dear boy?' the host inquired.

'Most willingly—whatever you wish!'

Our friend left the room, climbed the staircase, and returned with, in his hand, a tolerably bulky manuscript. This he proceeded to burn, leaf by leaf, on the hearth. As the first page flashed into flame, the young guest let out an involuntary cry of pain.

'Oh, what *is* it? What are you doing, dear Master?'

'We must all make mistakes, dear child. I am burning one of mine. Do not worry, I have been informed in no uncertain terms that it is a mistake, and I have come to a sorrowful agreement with that verdict.'

'But what are you incinerating? Not Toby's journal?'

The Master permitted himself a certain wryness in his look and tone as he replied, 'No, not poor Toby's journal, but a version, my own somewhat too decorated and Corinthian version of the events narrated therein.'

'I wish that you had let me read it,' said Hugh faintly, as the incineration proceeded. Our writer shook his massive head.

'No; it is better dispersed into air.'

'May I not, then, take Toby's version and offer it to my publisher?'

'No, my dear child. Not at this present time. Perhaps never. I have come, you see, to the conclusion—one which, I fear, should not have eluded me for so long—that it is too soon for Toby's journal to meet the eye of the public. The style is not appropriate for this present generation. A hundred years hence, perhaps—'

'But what, then, can you *do* for Toby?' Hugh's volatile sympathies, previously so jealous, so hostile to the figure of Toby, suddenly swung round and enlisted themselves in his favour. 'Shouldn't poor Toby have a look-in *somewhere*?'

'A "look-in", my beloved boy?'

'He wants his story published!'

The Master frowned. 'He must learn to be patient. Inexperienced writers are so often eager to rush into print—to see themselves published before a fitting occasion has arrived.—Even I myself have cause to regret a number of early effusions in magazines, before my taste was fully formed—'

'But poor Toby has no other chance!'

'I shall endeavour to reconcile poor Toby to the position as best I can. It will all, I daresay, as you yourself, dear boy, might possibly put it, "work out" . . .'

Nevertheless, after Hugh's departure, the Master, on several occasions, had cause to acknowledge to himself that, although he had put forth his best efforts to elucidate the situation and account for his decision, the notion, figment, entity, manifestation, or whatever it was, of Toby Lamb, remained unconvinced, unappeased.

The house, he felt, passed from scepticism and mistrust to an attitude that bordered on downright hostility.

A portrait, hanging on the wall, would momentarily, angrily, flash its eye at him. He would enter a room to find the arrangements in it subtly different—in some absurd, minuscule manner—from those he had left in it even if but a moment before. Neatly tied parcels, ready for dispatch, would be found unwrapped; he was reminded of how his father, who never possessed any proper adult control, would unwrap and show the children their Christmas gifts long before the day. 'Messages' were left him: in his bathroom, for instance—but such particulars are too trifling and ridiculous to recount. Drawers would be open and their contents disarranged—more particularly his desk drawers. Books would be shut which he had left open, and the markers withdrawn from the pages. Pages in

manuscripts would be misplaced. And—a phenomenon he most particularly disliked—when he sat down on a chair, he often observed that the seat felt *warm*, as if some other inmate of the house had but a moment before risen and left it vacant.—From a child, he had felt a marked distaste for sitting on a warm chair.

All these tiny occurrences, following one another, day after day, served, in the end, to make him feel most signally uncomfortable, lonely, and unwelcome in the house. He was more than commonly relieved to accept a series of autumn gales as sufficient excuse to transfer himself and his staff to London for the winter. Toby—who appeared by now to be his own age, or even older—seemed to be turning into some kind of undesirable elder brother, exigent and pleading by turns.

The house, our friend thought, wants people that it can *work on*—like the statue. It wishes to influence them. But I—most signally—wish to resist influence—to be free of it.

Although, he supposed, no one can, ever, be wholly free from influence. It is too much to ask.

In 1914 he decided to lend the house to any person who might, through force of circumstances, be in need of accommodation. He spent time in Rye only briefly, during July and August, and left again not long after the declaration of war. Young Burgess, his faithful servant, had gone to join the army; dear Hugh had departed to Russia as a war correspondent; Rye was now no place for our friend. And, in fact, soon after, he was denied even the possibility of going down there; as an American citizen, he would be obliged to apply for special permission to visit his property and to be under police supervision while there. Rye, being so close to the coast, was decreed a defence zone.

This our friend found hard to tolerate, and in 1915 he decided to become a British subject. Four signatures

were required on the application form: his were those of Sir Edmund Gosse, Librarian to the House of Lords, J.B. Pinker, our author's literary agent, Prothero, editor of the *Quarterly Review*, and Asquith, the Prime Minister, who all attested to his literacy and probity.

During the month of January 1915 the great mulberry tree in Lamb House garden blew down. In its fall it demolished the statue—'which be no great loss,' remarked Gammon the gardener, as reported by Fanny Prothero, a neighbour—'for the statue was that weathered and worn that it didn't look to be bigger than a ten-year-old boy. But the gaffer will miss the old tree surelye—he did dearly use to love a-sitting out under her—'

Now that our friend was a British national he might have returned to Rye. But the summer of 1915 found him ill, and reluctant to make a move: the idea of his garden without tree or statue distressed him painfully; as did the thought of expectant, constantly disappointed, Toby Lamb.

Previous to falling ill, our friend had been greatly occupied in visiting wounded soldiers who had been ferried back from the front to London hospitals; he had proved wonderfully, unexpectedly kind, patient, and sympathetic, listening to their stories, comfortably chatting with them, a perfect bedside companion. That summer his own poor wounded man, young Burgess, came back from the front, scarred by shrapnel and rendered permanently deaf; invalided out, he was able to return to his beloved master.

Who, meanwhile, was making another attempt to complete *The Sense of the Past*. 'It is for you, Toby,' he did his best to explain. 'A portrait of the hero, cut off and lost in a period that is not his own. A study of the terror of consciousness.'

But Toby remained unplacated, and the work went badly; it was never finished.

In October 1915 our friend paid a hasty visit to Lamb House. Many troubles were on his mind. In the bereaved garden, which he could hardly bear to survey, he carried out another great holocaust of documents; he 'burned up quantities of papers and photographs, cleared his drawers out', Alice James later reported. The distressing ceremony proved too much for our hero, and he suffered from violent heart palpitations and inability to breathe. Digitalis was required, and he had to return to London. 'Bustling is at an end forever for me now,' he wrote. His dear Hugh, just back from Russia, heard of this illness and was able to telephone to him from Cornwall.

On the 2nd of December he suffered a slight stroke, followed by another next day.

'So it has come at last, the Distinguished Thing,' he whispered.

He was not, however, to die immediately.

For three dreadful months he had to suffer varying degrees of helplessness, sometimes in bed, delirious and fevered, sometimes able to get up and sit in a chair, looking out at the River Thames and the barges on it; sometimes rational, sometimes rambling, at all times filled with mounting terror, hideously afraid of being thought mad by his visitors and servants; afraid of *being* mad.

He dictated letters, some of them from Napoleon to his sisters. Why did he identify with Napoleon? Was it in order to escape from his own painful consciousness? He complained about the absence of males in his entourage (though both his doctor and the faithful Burgess were continually at hand). 'The house is full of governesses and pastry-cooks,' he complained. 'Where is Toby? Why do I never see Toby?' Sometimes he believed himself to be in a hotel or on board a ship, or—now and then—in Ireland. He worried desperately about his manuscripts. 'And Toby's journal? Where is it?' he asked, over and

over. 'Is it back in the little closet? Did I put it there? Or was it burned up?'

But that, nobody could tell him.

He often had dreams of his sister—'a small, odd, sharp, crippled, chattering sister', who angrily rated him for not telling her story. 'I know—I know! You and William called me "that idle and useless young female whom we shall have to feed and clothe." You made me into what I am. All we can do now is die together,' she told him. And, on another day, 'Our friends are all putting out in a boat. We can only follow. Wide spaces are close at hand, and whisperings of release.'

'I shall be only too willing to set sail with you,' our hero told her, and she shouted, 'Sisters are of minor importance.'

Sometimes Toby did appear, briefly, asking about the papers he had burned, and he was obliged to explain, 'Aunt Kate helped me destroy them all; she said it was better that the children shouldn't see them.'

'Ah,' sighed Toby, and began to vanish.

'But don't go yet, my beloved boy; your visits are always so damnably short,' begged our poor friend. 'And indeed I do believe now that, for you, first-person narration was best. For some reason—I hardly know why—it failed for me in *The Sacred Fount*; but, for you, it is right. Oh, but I have seen you, Toby, so often, outside the window; why did you never, ever come in?'

Toby did not reply.

'I wish,' our friend one day told his sister-in-law Alice who had now, braving submarines, arrived in London (for she had long ago promised William that she would attend Henry at his end). 'I wish the boys had connections here.'

'*You* are their connection, Henry,' said Mrs James, thinking he referred to his nephews. 'They will try to follow you.'

'Tell them to *follow, to be faithful, to take me seriously.*'
And he mumbled something about Toby and Hugo.

But on another day, mysteriously, our writer exclaimed,
'Astounding little stepchild of God's astounding young
stepmother!'

On the 1st of January the Order of Merit, signed by the
King, was brought to his bedside. He said faintly, 'Turn
off the light so as to spare my blushes,' and added even
more faintly, 'I hope that poor Toby will not begrudge
it to me. Dear Toby—you shall have your recognition
during the course of this new century. As soon as I can
arrange it.'

On the 12th of January he begged, most piteously,
to go to Rye. 'I have *so many* things to arrange there.
I must make sure that the journal is safely back in the
closet. Burgess, will you tie a knot in my watch-chain to
remind me?'

In tears, Burgess promised that he would.

The night of the 24th of February was 'a night of
horror and terror'.

'The light is shrieking away outside,' he told his brother
William, 'and I am shrieking away inside. And I know that
just there, outside the door, squats the thing that has waited
for so long, it has come for me, and it is there, and it waits
out there in the long gallery, and soon I must go out and
confront it.'

William answered, 'No, but come with me. I promise
there will be no Mrs P. at the end of this tunnel.'

On the 28th of February our friend died.

'Several people who have seen the dead face are struck
with the likeness to Napoleon, which is certainly great,'
wrote his secretary, Miss Bosanquet.

Lamb House, bequeathed to his nephew Harry, was let,
firstly to an American lady, a Mrs Beevor, at a rent of

£120 a year. Finding the English climate uncongenial, she offered it to an artist, Robert Norton, who first shared it with and then offered it outright to the writer E.F. Benson.

The Figure in the Chair

3 · FRED

MY BROTHER ARTHUR and I, unattached and middle-aged persons, had, by the year 1919, fallen into the pleasant habit of sharing Lamb House.

Lamb House is not, as the name might suggest, located among fleecy flocks and green pasture-land, but sits snugly in the very centre of a little country-town: its rosy Georgian front looks towards the church and contains comfortable, square, panelled rooms; and, at the back, is this unsuspected acre of green lawn and flower beds, surrounded on all sides by high walls of mellow brick, over which peer the roofs and chimneys of neighbouring houses. The atmosphere of both house and garden is friendly and serene, distilled from the thoughts and personalities of the former generations who have lived there. Or so we thought, Arthur and I . . .

Our acquisition of the place had been, to me at any rate, quite unexpected.

It was almost twenty years since I had paid my first visit to the house, during the period when the old Master himself, Henry James, was still benignly in residence. For sixteen years he had been a friend of my family; my brother Arthur had first met him—'a small pale noticeable man with a short, pointed beard and large, piercingly observant eyes', wearing a white tall hat and an elegant light grey suit, at some luncheon party in 1884, and during the following year he visited our family and was told by my father (then Archbishop of Canterbury) the brief, germinal anecdote which would later be transmogrified and immortalised as *The Turn of the Screw*. I, on that occasion, was only sixteen. Six years later, when I had written half a novel, I was alarmed and embarrassed to find that my mother had sent the incomplete MS to the Master for his opinion—and not at all surprised when, in the course of several diplomatic letters, he conveyed, amiably but firmly, that it did not have the 'ferociously literary' qualities that might have earned his approval ... Its popular success when, as *Dodo*, it was published two years later must have confirmed his gloomiest feelings about public taste. He, however, continued to be invariably kindly and welcoming when one visited him in Rye.

After his death in 1916 I supposed that Lamb House would concern me no more, but in the pre-ordained decrees of fate, or, alternatively, in the fantastic hazards of a fortuitous world, it began at once to concern me more closely. The house was let to an American lady, and she, being obliged to winter in the south, left her housekeeper there and asked a friend of mine to occupy it if he wished, and he in turn asked me to share his tenancy.—Then Fate began to act with that capricious consistency that shows she means business. The remainder of the lease was offered to me; I could not take it then, but this offer seemed a sort of nudge, an aside, on the part of Fate, to indicate that she was attending, and meant that Lamb House was coming nearer. I passed the offer on to a friend of mine, who accepted it. But now the landlord of my villa in Capri told me that if I wanted to stay on I must purchase the place, which I had no intention of doing. Simultaneously my friend at Lamb House asked me, since he had to winter in the Riviera, if I would consider taking a sub-lease from October to the end of March.—I did not require much time for consideration.

Tremans, our family home, had been sold up after the death of our mother in 1918, and I needed a base.

Then, when the lease of Lamb House came up again for renewal, Arthur and I decided to share it. He, as Master of Magdalene College, spent the university terms in Cambridge at the Master's Lodge, but would use Lamb House in vacation time; I would have it for the rest of the year. This scheme suited us excellently; though we were fond of one another, we had little in common, but got on amicably when our paths ran together. Arthur, poor fellow, had for several years previously been afflicted by a long and black period of depression (to which most members of our family are regrettably prone) and Lamb House made, he found, a pleasant and cheerful haven where he could occupy himself in the writing of his copious diary (by his death it amounted to over four million words) and the compilation of those mellifluous books of meditations on spiritual topics which earned him such immense popularity with middle- and upper-class lady readers of a certain age.

A symptom of Arthur's intractable melancholia had been unhappy delusions: he thought his servants were starving to death because he had forgotten to pay them, or that he was surrounded by a horrible and offensive smell. I was, therefore, at first, faintly anxious about leaving him on his own in Lamb House, which bore the local reputation of being 'haunted'; however the same could be said of more than half the houses in little medieval Rye and, if there were a ghost, Arthur took no harm from it but, on the contrary, throve in its proximity: in 1923 he cancelled the power of attorney which he had, six years previously, felt it necessary to sign in case his reason totally collapsed; and he spent the vacation periods in Rye cheerfully and healthfully with students, or Percy Lubbock, or other professional friends, walking, bicycling, playing chess, reading, and writing.

In 1924 I ran across Hugh Walpole at a London literary 'do' given in honour of his latest book. (I do not recall which was the book in question; Hugh is a most prolific writer.) Such parties, which at one time had been a major feature of my life, I now attended less and less. In such a crush friends become acquaintances and talk with a roving eye to see who else is there; and acquaintances, glued together, look round to find a friend, and strangers struggle to get away from each other and find an acquaintance. But as Hugh had travelled all the way down from Cumberland for the affair, I felt that the least I could do was to put in an appearance.

'So you are inhabiting Lamb House!' he said. 'Are you happy there, you and Arthur?'

'Very happy indeed,' I told him.

'It seems queer to think of it without old Henry in residence; I used to visit him there so often at one time. But I am sure', he said kindly, 'that you and Arthur take very good care of it.'

'It takes care of *us*. It positively seemed to invite us.'

'Ah,' he said. 'Henry felt that too. It almost kidnapped him. And then, at the end, suddenly turned against him, so that he was afraid to stay there. And yet, poor Henry, he felt guilty at going off to die in London; felt the house would be lonely without him. Queer . . . And have you seen the ghost?'

None, I said, had as yet appeared. To which ghost did he refer?

'Why, the ghost of Toby Lamb.'

And Hugh proceeded to tell me about a manuscript that had once come to light in the house, and about Henry's painful and protracted doubts, scruples, and self-lacerations as to his duties and obligations in the matter.

'So what did he do with the manuscript?' I asked. 'In the end?'

'In the end? To the best of my knowledge, nothing,' said Hugh. 'For all I know, he put it back in the secret cupboard.'

Deeply interested, I asked if he had read this document. He had, he said, but confessed that now he could recall virtually nothing of its contents. 'After all, it was almost twenty years ago. I remember that the manuscript was in a horrible condition: handwritten, you know, in a vile crabbed script, besides being very faded and smoke-stained.'

'But the ghost—Toby—had asked for it to be published?'

'I think so ... it related the history of his sister Alice. I remember that, because of the coincidence of Henry's sister being another Alice. Something dreadful had happened. Very possibly I never finished reading it. Toby was lame, I remember ... Poor old Henry was in a great taking about it.'

'Why *didn't* he have it published?'

'I think his notion was that it might be distressing for the Lamb family to have some scandal in their history brought to light.'

I said that in my experience most families took a pride in such murky passages, provided they were sufficiently well removed into the past.

'Well,' reflected Hugh, 'another reason could, I suppose, have been professional jealousy. Old Henry had his share of that. You know: however encouraging he might be to a younger writer, there was always a sting in the tail. Perhaps he had an idea that Toby's story would catch the public fancy and outsell his own work; that kind of thing—'

I felt a pang of sympathy for Henry, remembering *Dodo*. 'I *wish* you could remember more—was it well written—?'

Unfortunately at this moment Hugh's publisher came up, with some important guest in tow, and we were separated. But later, as I was on the point of departure (the onset of arthritis, caused by a skating fall years before, was beginning to make all the standing about at literary parties more of a penance than a pleasure, while a hobbler on a stick does not add to general gaiety) Hugh caught me up in the doorway and said,

'I'll tell you who might be able to furnish more information about Toby's journal, and that's Edith Wharton. I've a notion the old boy showed it to her. Something he once said gave me that impression.'

'Edith Wharton! She lives in France these days, doesn't she?'

'You could write to her.'

'You have certainly filled me with a burning curiosity to read it. I shall go home and search for the hidden cupboard at once.'

But alas! when I did so, it was only to discover that the little secret compartment (located without the least difficulty behind a panel) was empty, and no mysterious document lay within; the Master had evidently reached some other decision about what to do with Toby's journal.

I wrote both to Edith Wharton and to the custodians of Henry James's unpublished papers at Harvard University. The latter wrote back to tell me that no such journal had been included among the documents entrusted to them at the Master's death. Edith Wharton's reply, when it came, was kind, but no more satisfactory.

My dear friend,

I am so sorry that I cannot be of more use to you. Yes, Henry *did* once give me such a story to read, but it was one of his own, based, I imagine, on the material in the original document, which at no point did he show me. Indeed, I was not even sure that it existed, though he dropped a hint or two about it. As for the actual events recorded, I am afraid it would have been almost impossible to deduce anything about those from Henry's story (which was called 'The Shade in the

Alley', I remember). The story was written very much in his 'later' style, full of what dear William described as gleams and innuendoes and felicitous verbal insinuations and prismatic interferences of light—in short, one couldn't make head or tail of what he was driving at! Something dreadful had happened to three people and poor Toby was heartbroken—that is positively all that I can tell you. I wish I could be of more help—

your sincere friend, Edith Wharton.

All this was highly unsatisfactory.

I would at this point have abandoned the quest—after all, Toby's ghost, if still around, had not manifested himself to us personally, and was being no trouble at all. I myself had, not long before, published *Miss Mapp* (which made enthusiastic use of my surroundings in delectable Rye) and was now busy working on *David of King's*, my life was well occupied and full of contentment. But my brother Arthur had now been bitten by the bug of curiosity; as a scholar, he was irked by the thought of that lost manuscript, and suggested that we should have recourse to mediumistic assistance. I was willing to indulge this fancy, and so we invited a brother and sister of our acquaintance, Thomas and Caroline Carrot, to come down to Rye and hold a seance. These young people were, just then, quite at the top of their interesting profession, and bore a high reputation for probity and integrity. Not only that, but they had achieved some remarkable results, obtaining well-attested and convincing messages from all sorts of well-known personalities on the Other Shore.

So Thomas and Caroline came to Lamb House, and a seance was arranged in the dining-room. All the thick velvet curtains were drawn, leaving the room in complete darkness, and Arthur and I, as well as a few interested neighbours, assembled round the table. The usual invocation to guides and angels was recited by Thomas, who then proceeded to go into a trance, while Caroline sat by with pencil and notebook ready to take down his utterances.

He began by making some strange gurgles, like an undervitalised soda-syphon; then a blue patch of light appeared on the ceiling and began to move rhythmically from side to side.

'Have you anything to tell us, Mr Carrot?' said I.

Greatly to Arthur's and my astonishment, Thomas then began to talk in a loud, hoarse, angry voice, undoubtedly that of our dead sister Maggie when she was afflicted by one of her delusional 'turns' and believed that she was besieged by terrible little creatures, not quite human. During one of these attacks poor Maggie went for our Mother, Ben, with a carving knife, and thereafter, for the last ten years of her life, had had to be immured in a Home at Roehampton.

'Why do you dress up as a man and pretend to be my mother?' bawled the familiar, furious voice. 'Why do you take that horrible woman into your bed?'—and a lot more unpleasant gibberish of the kind, casting utterly unjustified aspersions at our mother's lifelong friend Lucy Tait (who, heaven knows, would never have hurt a fly). Then another voice shouted, 'Get off the line, you tiresome hag!' and began talking about 'osculatory relaxations'. This, also, was the voice of a woman, but had a recognisable New England accent. 'The better part is to clothe oneself in neutral tints, to walk by still waters and possess one's soul in silence—or so they tell you!' this lady announced. 'Well, you poor fools—*don't you believe it!* There were fifty thousand surplus women in Boston—where are they now? I will tell you—they are all in this place—clogging up the entrances to the spirit world. So I am sincerely warning you: gather ye rosebuds while ye may, for there sure ain't any rosebuds here.' Then this voice too was superceded by another, soft but threatening, which clearly enunciated the words: '*If* you please, ladies—when you have finished gossiping, this is *my* garden, and I have a right to hang out my own washing on my own fence; but as you *are* here, perhaps you would kindly tell me if any of you have seen my brother Toby?'

A dead silence ensued. Then, all of a sudden, there came a tremendously loud rap on the wall just above my head.

Next moment we all of us realised that a thunderstorm must be raging outside, for there was a flash of lightning so dazzling that, despite the drawn curtains, it brilliantly lit the room, and it was followed by an earsplitting clap of thunder. During the second of time occupied by the flash I had noticed something very astonishing: on the heavy, lined velvet curtains covering the french window, a shadow was visible, that of a man, standing outside, leaning on two sticks. I sprang to the window and pulled back the draperies, but nobody was there. Another volley of thunder rattled the window-frames, and a deluge of rain was hurling down on the grass.

Thomas Carrot moved and stirred, returning slowly and drowsily to consciousness. 'Did I say anything interesting?' he asked.

We assured him with sincerity that, although the spirit we were hoping for had not 'come through', yet there had been various remarkable communications of other kinds. He nodded, rubbing his forehead. 'There are some powerful presences about,' he said. 'I'm very glad that you invited us. This house is full of possibilities. I need to rest now, but we'll conduct another seance in an hour or two.'

Arthur and I were both, I think, quite glad to get away from the dining-room, and, indeed, leave the house, which had assumed a rather oppressive atmosphere.

Normally, when I write, it is with great ease and

fluency, but just occasionally I feel that, although there is something I strongly wish to express, it is unable to make its way out, and sometimes there may be a tremendous struggle, which leaves me as exhausted as if I had taken a twenty-mile bicycle-ride, before the desired act of creation has been achieved, and the words are safely committed to paper. This was the way I felt after Carrot's seance, as if something close to me, or even within me, was struggling to find utterance and declare itself, but unable to do so.

'Phew!' said Arthur, as we strode down Mermaid Street through the downpour. We had tacitly agreed that, despite the appalling weather, we needed to get out of doors, at least for a short time.

'Do you think there was anything *in* all that?' said my brother at length, rather uncomfortably.

We walked as far as the Gun Gardens before I answered him, and stood there, side by side, regardless of the heavy rain, leaning against the outer wall, staring down across the marsh, what could be seen of it, and the steel-grey Rother, zigzagging its way to the sea.

'Well—' I answered him at last, temporising, 'as to "in" I don't know—but I'd say the first voice was undoubtedly that of our sister Maggie.'

'So would I,' he said. 'Then who were the others?'

'Alice James and Alice Lamb, perhaps? All the sisters putting their word in, do you think?'

'But *why*?'

'Why not?' I said reasonably. 'Because they didn't have the chance to do so during life?'

'Maggie had the chance,' he muttered. 'She did her excavations, she wrote books. In any case, why here? Why to us?'

'I suppose, because we invited them?'

He fell silent again, watching drops of water form and slide off the muzzle of a large cannon.

'*We* were invited,' he then burst out. 'Don't you feel so? The house sent for us.'

'It sent for Henry James too. Evidently it likes writers; literary men.'

'Or people of—' Arthur spoke with a certain awkwardness—'people of a—of a particular kind. Our family—I suppose nobody would deny that we are rather *queer*.'

'Queer; yes. But then, with two such incompatible parents—a father who was the Archbishop of Canterbury, rather too fond of flogging boys—'

'I once wrote the words "I hate Papa" on a bit of paper and buried it in the garden,' Arthur remembered.

'—And a mother as gentle and rational as Ben was—and she was only twelve years old, remember, when he told her that one day he was going to marry her, poor child—you'd *have* to expect the children of such a union to be—to be liable to fits of depression and mania, wholly averse to matrimony, or the opposite sex, obsessively addicted to writing—all that sort of thing. Wouldn't you?'

'The James family were pretty queer, too,' Arthur said, a little comforted.

'Not so odd as us. And there were only five of them. And *their* father wasn't an archbishop . . .'

'Then,' Arthur said, almost pleadingly, 'you think it all right for us to be the way we are?'

'My dear Arthur—you are sixty-four, I am fifty-nine—I don't think at our respective ages we are liable to change! And we have made a reasonable success of our lives—you are Master of Magdalene, Hugh was a Monsignor, I make a fair living from my books. And perhaps one day I shall become Mayor of Rye,' I added fancifully. 'But come on, dear old boy, we are both getting soaked through, and that isn't sensible.'

We returned to Lamb House and, after hot baths and tea with anchovy toast, the interrupted seance was resumed.

This time Caroline fell into a trance and took down dictated messages from Savonarola, Joan of Arc, and several other notabilities; messages of an innocuous and soothing kind, about the joys of existence on the Further Shore, where everybody was so kind and helpful to the newly arrived spirits. I could not help thinking that there must be at least a couple of different Further Shores; the messages we had received earlier seemed so wholly different in purport. But then I had said something like this in my book *Across the Stream* . . .

Now there came a pause, and then another terrifying loud rap on the ceiling; my terrier, Duff, let out a shrill nervous volley of barks. Caroline suddenly announced, in a man's deep voice: 'Fred. Is Fred there? I have a message for Fred.'

'Yes; what is it?' I asked, not alarmed so much as deeply interested. 'Fred is here listening.'

'Fred. Listen. Pay attention.'

Another pause. We waited. Then: 'This is Hugo Grainger speaking.'

Now I have a friend named Hugh Grainger (why he should suddenly have chosen to re-christen himself *Hugo* I could not imagine). At that particular moment I happened to know that Hugh was not Across the Great Divide, but healthily alive and playing golf at Brightlingsea (unless something dreadfully sudden had happened to him). Disappointed, therefore, but interested just the same (after all, it saved the cost of a telephone call) I said warily, 'Yes? Hullo, Hugh? What have you to tell me?'

'*Hugo*, not Hugh,' came the irritable answer. 'It is a message for you from my brother. From my blood brother,' he repeated with emphasis.

Now Hugh Grainger, to my certain knowledge, is an only child, so I said, even more cautiously, 'Yes, what is the message?'

'About the story. Forget it. It has caused enough grief. Forget it.'

'Easy to say that!' broke in another voice, angry, female. 'Why forget it? Why should the story not be told?'

'Forget it,' reiterated the first voice wearily. 'Toby says, forget it. Tell Henry, tell him—'

Then, upstairs, we heard the most almighty crash, as if half the house were falling down. We all sprang to our feet, Duff barking hysterically.

When we went to investigate the room above (which was my study, the Green Room) we found that my heavy walnut writing desk had been overturned on to its side, tipping papers, letters, and ink from a broken bottle, all over the floor.

'And what do you make of that?' said Arthur, when the mess had been cleaned up, and the two Carrots despatched, with thanks and liberal fees, back to Charing Cross on the seven o'clock train.

'Well, there certainly seem to be differing opinions on the Other Side.'

'I have always', said Arthur, 'maintained that the origins of psychic manifestations may be both human and diabolical—that there may be non-human entities of a demonic nature.'

'Such as Maggie's little non-human beings? And the small brown creatures that clairvoyant person saw at Tremans?'

'Yes; some such agency could be responsible for the apparent conflict in those communications.'

'That doesn't help us much further forward, does it? Even if it isn't just Maggie and Alice James being argumentative. I wonder if the Henry referred to was Henry James?'

'But if they wanted to get a message to him, why do it through *us*?' objected Arthur. 'After all, he is on the

Other Side already—has been for almost nine years.'

'He didn't believe in psychic survival. His ghost stories are all psychological ones,' I said, thinking of that terrifying tale, *The Jolly Corner*, where he meets his own evil double. 'Perhaps he is, somehow, incommunicado over there.'

'What precisely was the message, do you think?'

'Well—not to tell the story.'

I had already despatched a note to Hugh Grainger, asking why he should feel the need to direct psychic messages to me, and in a couple of days received a reply disclaiming any such intention. It was all decidedly odd; deuced rum, as Arthur observed.

The time had now come for him to return to Cambridge for the Lent term, and this, for the sake of his mental calm and tranquillity, I thought just as well. But, alas, the poor fellow had taken more harm than he realised from our wet walk and injudicious colloquy in the Gun Gardens. After his return to Magdalene he began to suffer from pains in his chest, and severe shivering fits. Pleurisy led on to a heart attack, and early in the summer he died. Summoned by telegram, I was able to be by his bed at the last.

'I'm glad you've come,' he whispered. 'Shall I take a message to Henry?'

The old impish smile, which I had not seen for years, reappeared on his face. Then he stopped breathing.

Saddened though I was by Arthur's death, I felt, I must confess, little sense of personal loss. We had grown apart; there were many friends of my own with whom I was on closer and warmer terms. Still, I was sad that before his end the enigma of Toby's journal and the Lamb House ghost had not been solved. That seance, I thought, had, on the whole, been a mistake; through its instrumentality something powerful and unpredictable had been unleashed which, up to then, had lain dormant and innocuous. Now it was loose . . .

There were odd manifestations about the house: doors banged, taps were found running, salt would be discovered spilled in a circle on the newly-laid and highly-polished dinner table; things like that. Nothing exactly menacing, but, on the other hand, not *friendly*; unsettling, tending to disquiet.

At this juncture I had a letter from a lady who called herself Madeline.

The real name of this person was Miriam Harvey, and she was a clairvoyante. I had never, I am thankful to say, met her, for she sounded to be a most tiresome and erratic lady, but for a short period, in fact during the time when I first moved in to Lamb House, she had bombarded me with letters over a number of months. She wrote that she had seen me in a vision, she sent me messages from my mother, Ben, who had died the year before, she addressed me as King Nebuchadnezzar, as Honour Bright, and as Kindly Light. In fact the poor dear sounded more than a little cracked, and yet every now and then one of her chatty, discursive letters (which were also liable to include mention of Winston Churchill, Bonham Carter, or Ali Baba and the Forty Thieves) would sound some disconcertingly true note. For instance she described my mother (whom she had never met) and all her surroundings with great accuracy.

Her letters had gradually tailed off and then stopped entirely. From this I had assumed, with some relief, that the poor lady had either died, or recovered her wits, or gone completely to seed. But now she wrote again:

Dear Kindly Light

Down in the gutter of a city street was a drop of water. Way up in the heaven a gentle sunbeam saw it; it leaped out of the azure sky down to the drop, kissed it, thrilled it through and through with new life, lifted it up higher and higher beyond the clouds, and one day left it as a flake of immaculate snow on a mountaintop.

The Inspiration of someone who saw provided we bring the inspiration of Apostolic zeal in salt, the fixed flash of that instant and intolerant Elightment, the Lightning made eternal as the Light.

The Church is a treasure in an earthen vessel. I could endure the Borgia Pope & St B Massacre—all but one thing—they are farcical.

I haven't heard voices since 1920. Almost to the day.

The elements. Are there only Earth, Fire, Water and Air, aren't there gases and secretions? God can 'raise men from stones'. Other things are compressed, distilled, rise above men. Why could not God display any phenomena? If a rose rises from a seed; how can anyone suppose there are no miracles—or why doesn't God obey us?

People who have no God take it out in action.

The voices tell me to tell you this, dear Honour Bright: Toby says to tell Henricus there is NO NEED to go further. H should rest in peace and Gather himself for his next apotheosis.

Mad Eline.

I was immensely startled by this letter. For how in the world would Madeline know about Toby and Henry?

'Thought transference,' said my friend Hugh Grainger, who happened to be staying in the house at the time. 'Like reincarnation, it does seem to happen. Every now and then the lady just happens to tune in on your wave-length.'

'Ye-es; it could be that; but what do you think started her up again, after such a long gap?'

Hugh reflected. He is a solid, sensible person, a doctor of obscure nervous complaints, and this makes him both exceptionally sensitive to other people's feelings, and sceptical of hysterical symptoms, or other phenomena that may be attributable to human causes. He therefore surprised me by saying: 'Well, you probably stirred things up, don't you suppose, by holding that seance. Up to that moment all the—layers of psychic strata that there must be in this house—let me see, when was it built?'

'In 1721—but of course there was a building here before that date.'

'Well, there you are, just think what a lot of events, some of them fairly dramatic no doubt, must have taken place here during the course of those two hundred years. You, with your seance, did something like sinking an artesian well, disturbing and breaking through all the different strata. And not surprisingly you get a gusher.'

'I think you are mixing your metaphors, Hugh. But I see what you mean. It seems queer, though, that elements come in from outside—Alice James, after all, never was here. Nor was our sister Maggie. Nor was "Madeline".'

'But bodily location doesn't have any importance in the spirit world,' he pointed out briskly. 'After all, Savonarola and Joan of Arc weren't here either; and yet they seemed to feel quite at liberty to send you messages. I think in a case like this where there is a kind of psychic "focus" other elements probably get sucked in from further off; it's a bit like a tornado.'

'I most sincerely hope not!'

'Arthur's death may have caused additional disturbance; I suppose the death of anybody connected with an affair like this will be bound subtly to alter the balance as between this side and the Other Side.'

'Well,' I said, 'one thing Arthur *doesn't* seem to have been able to do is to pass on that message to poor old Henry; if Toby still feels it necessary to "come through" to me via Madeline.'

'It's a most interesting problem,' said Hugh, scraping in his pipe, which had gone out. 'How to get a message from one spook to another spook.'

'Do you think we should hold another seance?' I suggested doubtfully.

'No,' said Hugh, 'I'm averse to seances. There's always an element of charlatanism about them which I find distasteful. No, I'll give it some thought. But, in the meantime, perhaps you'll find that the manifestations die down spontaneously. Like bees, you know, after the hive is disturbed.'

In fact, this comforting hypothesis appeared to be a correct assessment of the situation, for, during the next three or four years, although there might, from time to time, be the odd manifestation, mirrors falling from walls, bowls of junket mysteriously overturned, small pieces of paper with inscrutable messages found in places and at times where no human agency could have placed them—nothing of a serious or violent nature took place; the spirits that inhabited, or occasionally took a fancy to visit, Lamb House, appeared to be quiescent, and troubled us hardly at all.

Hugh's analogy of a beehive seemed a happy one: the bees were there, gently buzzing, but they went about their business, as we about ours, and each party left the other undisturbed.

Beyond the west end of the Lamb House property lay a secret little enclave, a small square plot of ground surrounded by brick walls. Henry James, years ago, had bought it, to obviate the danger of anybody ever building a house on the site. He had then leased it to a neighbour in Mermaid Street who incorporated the plot in his own garden. But that neighbour had now died, and the use of the property therefore reverted to me. The first thing I did was to open a hole in the wall between it and my garden, to see what use could be made of the place.—I never saw a more dejected spot. There was an aged pear tree, a gnarled ampelopsis, a series of rubbish heaps, some neglected flower-beds full of weeds, and bushels of snails.

At once I saw what could be made of it, a secret garden, and withal an outdoor sitting-room, of which no inch would be visible from the surface of the earth.

Gradually, in the succeeding years, this was done. The enclosed square was turfed, with flower-beds round the walls, against which I planted Mermaid roses. In the centre of the turf I erected a pillar, built of old bricks, and on it a marble bust of the young Augustus, bought in Rye. In the north corner I constructed a shelter, twelve-feet square with tiled floor and wooden walls, open on two sides to the garden. In summer I furnished this with a writing-table, and on its wall hung an oblong mirror so that, sitting at work, I could see the reflection of the garden framed in it. Out of doors the eye wanders, but by this device it is forced to concentrate on what is framed, and the picture of the sunlit beds seen in the shadowed mirror glowed with an added brilliance.

And one day, sitting at my writing-table, glancing up into my mirror, I saw the reflection of a man who stood with his back to me, in the sunny garden, close beside my marble bust.

As I remained motionless, riveted with surprise—for I had heard no voice or step, had thought I was completely alone in the place—he, with a sudden petulant violence, picked up the heavy bust and hurled it on to the grass.

Outraged and astonished, I spun round—*and there was nobody in the garden.* Only my poor bust lay with its nose buried in a clump of forget-me-nots.

I rose, as quickly as I was able—for by this time the arthritis in my hip had made me exceedingly lame—and hobbled to the door which led from the secret garden into the garden proper. But, as I had expected, there was nobody in that garden either. The agency that had picked up my bust (which must have weighed at least sixty pounds) and hurled it with such angry force was no human one.

'What did he look like?' asked Hugh, who (summoned by telegram) came without delay and evinced the most acute interest in my story. The bust had been left lying *in situ* until his arrival; he, now, with the help of my gardener, carefully lifted it up, not without difficulty, and restored it to its former position.

'That is what is so frustrating! I never saw his face! He had his back turned to me. But he was dressed in black—of that I am certain—and had a black hat, or cap, on his head.'

'I have been thinking hard, on the way here,' said Hugh. 'I suppose you stirred up psychic activity again by opening up that garden. What would you say now to trying exorcism?'

'*Exorcism?* Well—I don't know, my dear fellow,' I began, rather doubtfully.

'It can't do harm—and *might* do good.' Hugh is a Catholic, and, like most of those born into the faith, tempers his with a vigorous scepticism, quite unlike my own brother Hugh, who, as a convert, treated all his acquired beliefs with the utmost seriousness.

'Exorcism?' I repeated. 'Don't you think that might—might just stir up all the hornets again?'

'Well, let us see. Let's wait a few days first.'

It was summertime, and Hugh had come prepared to loaf, as he put it, so we went for drives in his motor-car, lunched with friends at Dover, visited Walmer Castle and Bodiam, or, on chilly days, lit a fire in the Garden Room and did *The Times* crossword puzzle between us. And we watched; unobtrusively, vigilantly, ceaselessly, we watched. On two further occasions I saw the *revenant*:

once, as before, in the secret garden mirror, staring down at the bust (but this time he did not disturb it) once, walking through the arched doorway from the main garden to the secret one. And Hugh saw him, standing on the grass, pensively studying the patch of ground where the old mulberry tree used to grow . . .

One thing these sightings all had in common: we never saw his face. The spectre's back was always firmly turned away.

'Why is that, do you suppose?' said Hugh. 'Just because he has an unsociable nature? Or because his face would frighten us so . . . ?'

The thought gave me a sudden thrill of alarm. And when Hugh again proposed that we should fetch in an exorcist, I, at last, gave my reluctant agreement.

So Father Gabriel Comberbatch was brought down to Rye—he was a voluble little character with ingenuous blue eyes and a kind of fairy-ring of thistledown hair. But he seemed to know his job and set about the ritual in the most businesslike way. It had been agreed that the secret garden was the most appropriate location, since the ghost had now been seen there three times. Father Gabriel had equipped himself with holy water and a candle; he had various books, and wore his cotta and stole. Hugh acted as his assistant. Prayers were said, and a psalm—and then he bade the troubled spirit depart from that place, commanding it in the name of the Mysteries, the Incarnation, and the Passion. He also read from the gospels, that passage in which authority was given to the church to cast out unclean spirits.

After which he called out, 'Flee, ye adverse hosts. Begone from this place!'

Then, in Latin, he began, 'Exorcizo te—' for the third invocation.

He had chosen to perform his ceremony at sunset; for that was the time, he said, when the forces of light are still strong, and the things of the dark have not yet attained their greatest power.

During the various prayers, the light had been fading steadily; now, as if some stage manager had clapped his hands, night fell—and I use the word *fell* advisedly, as it seemed to happen: in one swift movement, light was withdrawn, and darkness was complete. The candle, after a last faint flicker, went out; far in the distance, to the west, we heard a growl of thunder.

'There!' said Father Gabriel cheerfully. 'That went off without a hitch, I flatter myself! I don't imagine you'll have any more problems in here now.'

And he allowed us to escort him back to the house, Hugh carrying the vessel with the holy water, and I the books. Once, Father Gabriel stumbled, for it was quite remarkably dark.

Over supper—at which he praised my cook's soufflé—he said that he did not anticipate any more trouble in the little garden. That place was now quite effectively cleansed of supernatural emanations. 'They can't stand Luke 9:1! Now, I think I should really be aiming for the nine-fifteen train . . .'

We pressed him to stay the night, but he said he was due next morning early for an exorcism at Aldeburgh—'Oh, a most obstinate, intractable case of possession—' and we could not alter his decision. So Hugh and I walked him down to the station.

The storm, which had been muttering quietly all evening, now declared its official opening, as it were, with one incandescent violet-coloured stroke of lightning, silhouetting the whole town, its mound of clustered roofs and church-tower, against a livid sky. We always do get very remarkable thunderstorms at Rye, and this promised to be a notable one; Father Gabriel said he was really sorry not to be able to stay for it.

Hugh and I walked back to Lamb House in silence. If we had tried to speak, we would have had precious little chance of hearing one another; the thunder was really making a devil of a racket. I was thinking about exorcism, casting out devils; was that spirit really a devil?

Just as we reached the wide Georgian door, the heavens opened and rain fell in torrents; we fled inside, just in time.

My man, Charlie, had left a fire burning and a tray of drinks in my upstairs study. From there we had an excellent view of the storm, which was spectacular.

And, as we stood by the window with glasses in our hands, a sudden preternaturally violent and livid glare of lightning, laying bare the whole garden, lawn, flowerbeds, and trees, with the clarity of a photographic print, revealed something more than wet grass and glittering foliage: a dark figure standing isolated on the far side of the lawn, in the shelter of the trees there.—Not that the trees would afford much shelter, I thought; every leaf, every twig, every blade of grass must be drenched and dripping.

'Did you see that?' whispered Hugh, in the hush before the thunderclap.

I nodded, forgetting that he could not see me; a sudden gust of wind had driven the flame of our lamp to a tiny point.

'Father Gabriel's exorcism doesn't seem to have been very effective.'

'All he did was drive it out of the secret garden into the big one.'

'Wait—look—'

Another flash flung brilliant light into every corner of the garden. And it also showed us that the figure had moved, it was now halfway across the lawn towards the house. I could not help being reminded of a sinister game my brothers and sisters had played when young in Cornwall. It was called Grandmother's Footsteps. You have to move forward so as to touch somebody, but you have to move without being seen doing so . . .

'It's coming towards the house,' announced Hugh unnecessarily. 'Did you get a glimpse of its face that time?'

'No.'

'Well: I did.' He did not enlarge on that. Nor did I ask him to.

Another flash showed us the figure, now directly below us, approaching the french window.

From where we stood we could not see the door open, but we heard it do so, in a moment, and felt a cold gust of displaced air blow upwards through the silent house.

'It has come inside,' said Hugh. 'It's come in—ha!—out of the rain.'

Another glare showed us each other's faces, from which we took little comfort.

'Well—we can't just stay here,' I said boldly, trying to conceal my fear, and ran down the stairs, with Hugh close behind. An icy wet wind blew in through the dining-room. I crossed it, grabbed the wildly swinging door, and pulled it towards me until the latch clicked.

Somehow it seemed important to do that, regardless of *what* I might be shutting into the house with us.

Behind me I heard Hugh give a kind of groaning gasp, and then he fainted, his considerable weight falling with a thud full-length on the floor. Through the door I then heard, unmistakably, a slow, heavy footstep ascending the stair.

'*Stop!*' I shouted foolishly. 'I order you to stop—by—by the Powers of Light!'

But the footstep went heavily on its way.

I knew that I had to go after it. If I did not—if I allowed it unchecked, undisputed access to the house—I should never be able to respect myself again, never have any peace of mind. Leaving poor Hugh inert on the carpet, I followed, I climbed the stair and went, trembling uncontrollably, into the Green Room, where the light still burned, flickeringly and dim. And there, by this faint and doubtful light, I at last confronted the apparition and beheld its countenance.

It was a face of unimaginable horror.

I have myself described dreadful visages, in various of my stories; in *The Luck of the Vails*, for instance, Uncle Francis had a face that by occasional, sudden change would become 'scarce human ... the lips drawn back from the mouth till the gums appeared ... the pleasant rosiness of the face was blotched and mottled with patches of white and purple'—but I had never, never, in my wildest imaginings, conceived one-tenth of the awfulness of the physiognomy that now confronted me. The worst feature, perhaps, was that *it was familiar; I had seen it before.* Where or how this was so, I knew not; but in its grotesque hideousness, its evil odiousness, it was as well known to me as my own appearance in my shaving-mirror. Making an effort like that of a man dragging himself from a quicksand, I averted my eyes from the atrocious face, and saw that the figure, which was dressed in ordinary black clothes, lacked two fingers on one of its hands; these were reduced to stumps, as if they had been shot away.

'Leave my house!' I commanded it hoarsely. 'Leave my house, you foul and infernal being. Begone from here!'

A husky and murmured reply seemed to issue from it. 'But this is my house too!'

Without heeding my command, the being turned away and sat on a chair.

Some kind of healthy, burning rage filled me then. Words came into my mouth. I shouted: *'You're afraid of me, you coward! I know it! I can see the sweat on your brow!'* and I strode round the chair, obliterating, by this action, my own deadly fear, so as to confront the apparition once more, so as to look it in the face.

And now, to my utter astonishment, the face I saw was wholly different, had changed with a speed similar to that of my invented Uncle Francis. The face that confronted me now had lineaments as kindly and well known as any member of my family, bore, indeed, a fond and paternal expression, though one that was, at the same time, deeply sad.

'Henry! My dear Master!'

For the face was that of the former owner of Lamb House.

'My boy—my dear boy—' he murmured, after a moment, in a voice that seemed to hold a whole lifetime of lamentation in its mellifluous cadences. And then, gathering a little force, 'How—how did I come to be here?'

'You were anxious—you were concerned—' I said. 'About Toby's journal—'

'Toby's journal—ah, yes.' A look of even deeper anguish crossed the large countenance. 'That boy. That poor boy. But at least—he never had to leave his home. He was not dragged back and forth across the Atlantic.' Then, seeming to recollect himself, he perturbedly said, 'My dear—that's the trouble. I don't know what I did with it. I think I concealed it somewhere—I am almost positive that I did not burn it—'

'Cher Maître,' I told him, 'please, listen—*it doesn't matter*. Toby has changed his mind about it. He left a message for you: "Forget the story." He has, I understand, lost interest in it.'

Did I hear a faint mutter of thunder outside? A faint cry of outrage in the tones of Alice Lamb? If so it quickly died away.

The Master's reaction was positive and instantaneous.

'He said that? Toby did? He really meant it? Oh, the blessed, blessed relief . . .' I thought I saw a tear sparkle on his cheek. He murmured to himself, 'Poor boy—poor boy—to deprive him of his chance of immortality; I know how hard, how very hard that is—to feel that your work has sunk without a trace—even when you know, yourself, that it is not without merit—'

His words, I must confess, gave me a pang. For, latterly, I had come, more and more, to the opposite conclusion about my own work. I had not, I knew, gone deep enough in my novels. They were shallow things. I had merely turned over and over the same spadeful of earth. I would never, I knew now in my heart, come anywhere near to rivalling the Old Master, even if the number of books I wrote rose into the hundreds. And yet they sold well, and were popular.

'Master,' I assured him, 'your work is better known, by far, now, than it was in your lifetime. Your books are never out of print. You are read and studied; your fame grows with every year. In time to come, hundreds of volumes of biography and criticism will recall you—there is talk of setting up a memorial stone on this very house—your name will never die—'

A slow, ineffable smile grew on his face. The eyes beamed at me wonderfully.

'My boy—are you really sure of that?'

'Sure as that the sun will rise tomorrow.'

'*Thank you*,' he said, 'thank you, thank you . . .'

And, as the words faded, he faded too, until I was alone in the room, with the faint light from the guttering lamp, and the growing light of a new day.

At a slow and painful pace I limped down the stairs to Hugh, who was gradually and wincingly pulling himself to his feet. And I told him what had befallen.

'Somehow,' I said, 'somehow I don't believe we shall be troubled here by hauntings any more.'

'But the house *likes* ghosts,' Hugh argued obstinately. 'It wants ghosts. What about Alice Lamb? And the one who called himself Hugo? What about those other voices that we heard?'

'Oh well. Perhaps they will, by and by, gather themselves together again and float back. But not, I fancy, in our time. Perhaps you and I, Hugh, will be the next pair of ghosts to take over the lease. Perhaps *we* shall be occupying the secret garden here in the year 2030!'

'Perhaps we shall!' said Hugh.

But so far I have been proved right. Not a spook, not a spirit, has come to trouble our peace up to the present day. And Toby's manuscript has never come to light . . .